THE BOOK OF DEMONS

KEVIN MOORE

www.KevinMoorePublishing.com

ISBN: 978-1-95386553-3 (Paperback)
ISBN: 978-1-95386554-0 (eBook)
ISBN: 978-1-95386555-7 (Audiobook)

Library of Congress Control Number: 2022902406

Books Fluent
3014 Dauphine Street
New Orleans, LA
70117

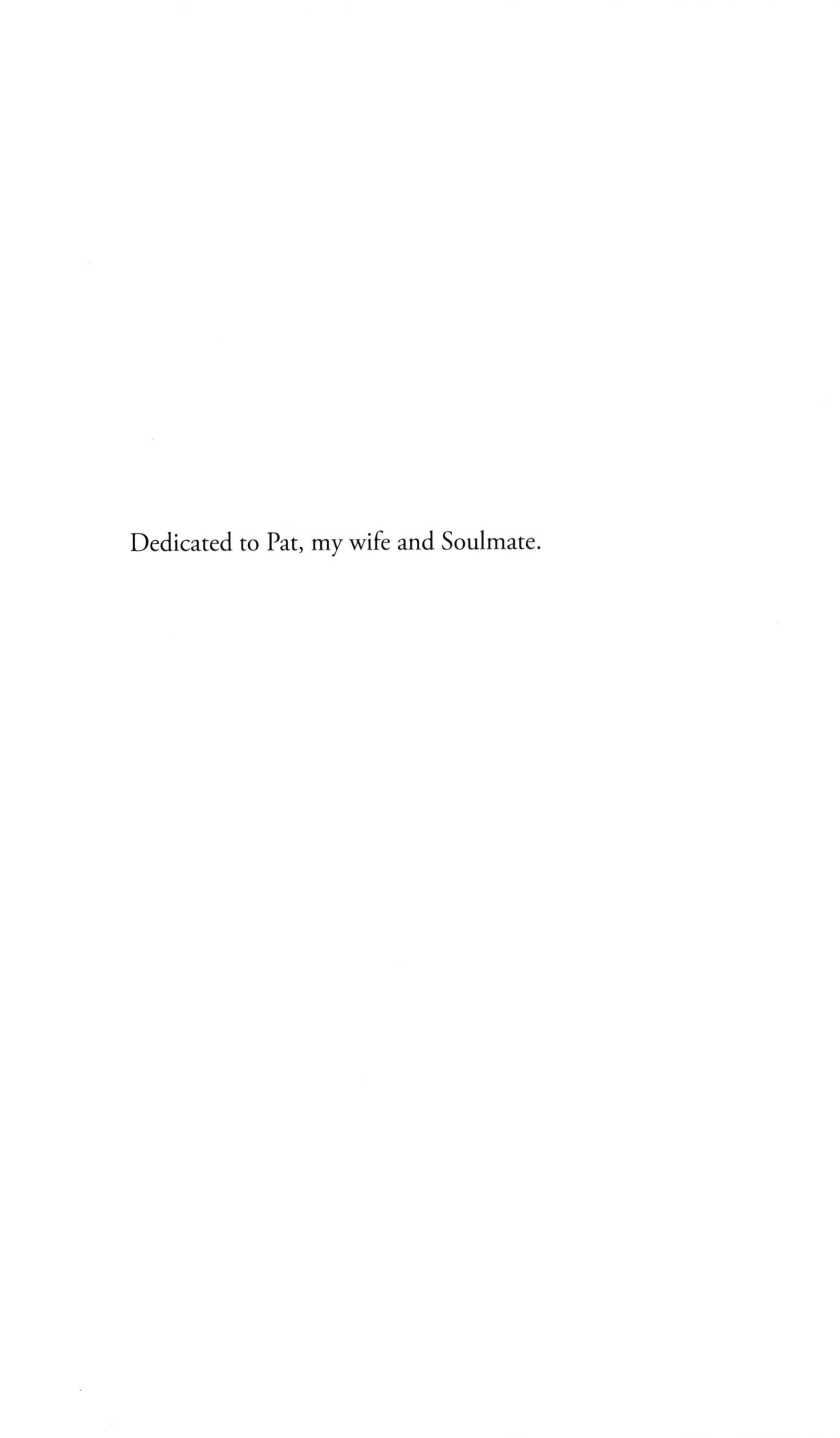

Dedicated to Pat, my wife and Soulmate.

PHILIPS

Mr. Philips—Philip—did not always go by that name. Before he was able to shapeshift, he was Seymore Hunter, a good-looking man on the other side of thirty working in a haberdashery before World War II broke out in England. His goal was to leave London for Los Angeles and become a film star. At first, Seymore was more into blackmail than black magic. Then he met Dr. Cecil Dels. Dels was a fancy dresser who became a regular customer and held deep knowledge of numerology, astrology, and Enochian magic. All of this was fascinating to Seymore, but Dr. Dels' involvement in black magic and the occult really made Seymore come alive. Seymore believed in nothing really, other than the magic of sleight of hand. Since he was nine, he was able to lift wallets without ever getting caught. Dels offered a completely different education from anything Seymore had been taught in school or life; he became a sponge. Not because he believed in any of it but because he felt it could be a great tool to make money, especially when he arrived in America.

Dels had invited Seymore to be his guest at the very famous, but hush-hush séance of Alice Walker. Alice was an expat American with a dubious heritage, having been married to an Eastern European count and a German duke. A widow twice over, she resided in London, where her mystique was further enhanced by the many wealthy people who came to her home hoping to contact dead relatives or place spells on enemies. It was all donation-based, but if you wanted to be invited back or needed a reading, your donations would be very well-placed.

Alice Walker did not greet guests when they arrived. Instead, her staff handled it. Drinks were simple in nature—a French 75, sherry, whisky, or a glass of Bordeaux. Guests were directed to the main drawing room and its high ceilings with crown molding, a beautiful large Venetian crystal Chandelier, and white and black marble flooring. Murals covered the walls instead of paintings. The women sat at the end of the couches and chairs, sipping their drinks. The men stood by the stone fireplace, which was lit, even though it was not a cold night.

Seymore felt out of place. He wandered around the parlor, sipping his wine, then made his way back to the entry and the only painting that hung on the walls. It depicted a beautiful woman standing alone in a garden. There was nothing unusual or even special about it until Seymore noticed the woman's shadow. It was not close enough to her body to be her own. Knowing nothing of art, he thought of it as a mistake by the artist.

"It's not a mistake. It's learning how to use shadow energy to your advantage. To do your bidding." The voice was firm, strong, deep. Southern?

Alice Walker. He knew the moment he laid eyes on her his life would change.

She was not tall, but her hair was dark, as were her eyes. Not beautiful but very attractive. Seymore stood there, speechless.

"You're very good looking. As good looking as any movie star." She said it with no smile or hint of flirtation.

"And you..."

She stopped him before he could return the compliment. "Let's join the others. We can get to know each other later."

The party moved into a room in the middle of the house so removed from the living area that you could get lost trying to find it or leave it, which was the idea. On a large round table sat a small bowl of soup, a small glass of sherry, and three candles in the center. There were twelve guests; Seymore learned later that the ideal number was to be divisible by three. A late cancellation allowed Dels to invite him in order to get the number right. Serendipity. Once the doors closed, the room appeared to be soundproof. Alice Walker lit the candles, while the guests were told to place their left hands up and right hands down on those of their neighbors. Seymore watched her intently, looking for tricks or theater. There were none.

It was all very understated until the spirit of Moses began to move through Alice Walker. The energy in the room changed once Moses, through Alice, began to speak. She immediately zeroed in on the couple who had been talking to Dels earlier in the evening. Her voice changed slightly, the accent and speech pattern most notably. Moses-through-Alice began giving very specific insights, conveying information from the man's mother. The private information made him highly emotional. Several others at the table were given minor messages before Alice ended her channeling.

The guests were not encouraged to linger. They left their offerings in a crystal bowl, whispering to one another about how wonderful the evening was. No verbal thanks to Alice was needed, nor expected; their gratitude was reflected in their gift. Seymore looked to Dels, who was meandering in the foyer.

Alice touched Seymore's arm. "A glass of wine?"

She guided Seymore into the large drawing room and poured them both a glass of Bordeaux. "Do you like art, Mr. Hunter?"

"Yes, but my art education is limited." As an afterthought, he added, "Call me Seymore."

She led him to the mural dominating the drawing room. "Would you like me to tell you about the murals?"

"It's beautiful, but may I ask you, why murals?"

Earlier in the evening, Alice had been all business; now she was relaxed, charming. "Why not murals?"

"Well." He paused, trying to choose his words. "I would think a painting would have more value."

"You are talking monetary value."

Of course, Seymore thought, *what other value is there?*

"These are what are known as architectural style or illusionistic images. They were from the Romans–found in Pompeii."

Seymore sipped his wine while looking around the room at the murals. "They are stunning."

"Yes," Alice said, spinning around to view them herself.

She was not acting like a mysterious channeler. He knew women like this—from a distance. They were much smarter than the men in the room but felt they needed to keep a level of gaiety, so they didn't lose their femininity.

"It's to trick the viewer," she said, as if she was reading Seymore's mind.

He took a step back. "What is?"

"The style of painting. It is intended to shift the eye of the observer. They are looking outside at a fountain, or a hillside in the distance, not fully realizing that they are still in a small room."

Seymore stood in front of the mural. There was no fountain outside, no distant landscape. The scene was outside on the patio, the sun was a tarot card, and there was a man—his eyes only white— looking at a beautiful woman with mysterious symbols on her gown.

Seymore finished his wine. "Is he blinded by her beauty?"

"Pour yourself another glass."

Seymore walked to the bar and realized the servers hired by Alice were gone. After pouring the wine, he asked, "Well, is he?"

Alice looked at the painting. "Could be. He's blinded by something." She sat on the couch, joined by Seymore.

"Are these particular murals painted to create a feeling of mysticism?" he asked. She smiled but did not answer. "And the canvas with the shadow? Does all the art set the mood for your guests?"

Alice curled up on the sofa, draping her hand on the back, close to his shoulder. He looked at her and smiled, then picked up her hand, pretending to read her palm.

"What do you see?" she asked.

Seymore caressed her hand. "Unlimited happiness and adventure." He kissed her palm gently. "So soft."

Alice caressed his face in turn. "And what does this unlimited happiness look like?"

He smiled. "It must be discovered."

She gently slid her finger across his lips. They stared intensely into each other's eyes. Seymore leaned in, captivated, then kissed her very slowly, for a long time. She stood and looked at him on the couch, then bent over, her hands holding his face. "I am the first room at the top of the stairs. Come up in ten minutes."

Alice's hands moved slowly from his face, lingering on his neck and shoulders before she left the room. Seymore watched her eagerly.

He jumped to his feet, excited at the feast awaiting him. He paced the room and poured more wine but never drank it. He walked to the fireplace then stood in front of the painting with the shadow, puzzled, sure the shadow had moved. After waiting a moment, he checked his watch and immediately headed for the stairs.

Seymore Hunter could not get enough of Alice. He found himself spending more and more time with her. He quickly grew jealous of the relationship between Alice and Cecil Dels—a very close, very secretive relationship. Although Seymore was her lover, he was the outsider when the three were together. They'd travel to the English countryside, then to Paris, and eventually to Romania. Alice and Dels were in search of mystics; the occult; and more importantly, the fountain of youth. Along the way, she conducted readings, while Dels would offer financial or political tips that were really breadcrumbs to get little pieces of information to help Alice with the readings and perhaps help Dels as a financial advisor back in London. There were always money and contacts to be made, and they always figured out ways to make them.

Meanwhile, Alice laid out small gestures of seduction for Seymore. She gave him little gifts of chocolate, a man's scarf, fancy writing paper, a tiny bottle of cologne. She explained to him about the shadow in the painting, alluding to its magic that she could use to control the shadow to lean in and get information on people who came for readings. In that way, she learned their secrets and their fears. He found much of this to be mad, but Alice did possess insight. He wasn't quite sure what Dels and Alice were after, though. In the beginning, he thought they wanted him for sex, perhaps a ménage à trois. But it never came up. Both were of a certain age and seemingly wanted to turn back time, or at least pause it. The trip to Romania was supposed to uncover an elixir of some sort that would help them do just that.

When they arrived in Romania, a virus was breaking out in Europe and Russia. People were very nervous at how fast and deadly the virus seemed. They began whispering the word "pandemic." Memories of the Spanish flu and the millions killed by it created suspicion of anyone with a cough or a sneeze. If that wasn't enough to worry about, concerns about Germany rearming itself triggered an even higher level of paranoia. People were suspicious of everything and everyone.

None of this seemed to bother Dels or Alice.

The three spent the first night in Romania, having dinner at the Count and Countess Vladimir's house. The Count and Countess were rumored to be decedents of Count Kazikli Voyvoda, who may or may not have been the inspiration for Count Dracula. Seymore found all of it great theater. Everyone was so dramatic. He also found himself in love both with Alice and the excitement she provided.

As he listened, he found himself much more interested in their upcoming trip to Pestera Lilicalor than anything the Count and Countess had to say. Pestera Lilicalor was known as the "Bat Caves." After being very evasive, Alice finally confided in him over drinks in their private suite that they were going with a guide to find a bat species that, when eaten, prevented aging and increased sexual energy. She assured him that he did not need any more sexual energy. "But wouldn't you love to look and feel like you do now for the next twenty years?"

She moved her lips to his ear. "You have to eat the bat while it is still alive in order for it to work, and it needs to be the heart or liver," she whispered.

Seymore could hardly believe his good fortune. This was much more exciting than anything he had done prior to meeting her. He was going from trying to match ties at the men's clothing store to the fountain of youth.

It was a long drive to the caves. As Seymore sat in the front seat with the guide, he noticed Dels had been moving slower all morning; at first, Seymore thought it was because of the early start. However, during the drive, he began noticing a change in Dels' skin and speech. The closer they got to the cave, the more lethargic Dels became. They did not speak about what they knew: Dels was infected with the mysterious virus. Alice wrapped her scarf around her face, moving as far away from him as possible in the back seat. Seymore kept his window down. The guide spoke broken English and spent a good deal of his time smoking cigarettes.

By the time they arrived at the caves, Dels was sweating through his clothes and had fallen into a deep sleep. Neither Alice, Seymore, nor the guide spoke of changing plans and getting him to a doctor. They simply laid him down on the back seat; took the cages, nets, water, flashlights, and other supplies from the trunk of the car; and headed into the caves.

Inside, the interior walls looked like gray granite through the darkness. The damp caves smelled musty, earthy. The guide carried a gun. "Why the gun? Do bats attack?" Seymore asked.

"Other poachers." Through his teeth, a cigarette hanging from his lips, the guide's accent sounded like a bad interpretation of Dracula in a B movie. His voice echoed off the walls of the cave.

Seymore needed to keep his wits and directional aptitude; the gun was making him suspicious. Not to mention Dels being left in the car with a possible killer virus. What if he took their money and left them in the cave to die? There were so many turns and smaller caves into which they kept walking. Not to mention Seymore's anxiety about bats. He went on high alert.

Stepping into another section of the cave, Seymore noticed light from another entrance. "Why didn't we come in that way?"

"Must travel over mountain," the guide replied.

As they walked deeper into the caves, the smell of earth and soil was replaced with the scent of urine and guano. Before Seymore had a chance to ask about it, the guide pointed up. Hundreds of black and brown bats stuck to the ceiling. They made a lot of noise; apparently, bats like to talk, with a language of their own. They even fight over sleeping position, mating partners, and food—and sometimes, just for the fun of it.

Seymore waited for direction as the guide began setting up the cages. Alice watched from a distance with apparently no fear; though, Seymore thought she looked pallid.

The guide took out a long BB gun and another object that looked like a water pistol and began shinning his light onto the wall. It started slowly, like a choreographed dance building into a steady movement. The bats began to move, to make noise. As if to announce the arrival of divinity, they began fluttering around in a frenzy. Slowly, from behind the wall of black bats, an albino bat emerged, glowing in the dark. Its arterial system was completely visible, as was its beating heart. All three gasped at the sheer magic of the creature.

The guide saw an opportunity for an even larger payday. "This is a mystical creature, only in folklore," he said. "Ten times more powerful than the ones we came here for."

He picked up the water gun and pointed it at the bats, handing Seymore and Alice nets.

"Is that water?" Seymore asked.

"No. It is a compound that will paralyze a small mammal. Be ready."

With one blast, the liquid hit the albino bat, as well as several others. One immediately fell directly at their feet, but the albino flew directly at the guide in Kamikaze fashion, followed by an army of bats. Seymore and Alice swung their nets, with Alice catching the albino and Seymore getting a black and brown bat. Within moments, mayhem ensued. The bats did the exact opposite of their typical behavioral response—they attacked! Panicking, Alice and Seymore hurriedly tried to get the bats into the two cages. The plan was for the albino to go in one cage alone, with the others in the second cage. Seymore packed his two bats into the cage quickly.

He turned to find Alice struggling. Immediately, he went to help and found her extremely pale and sweaty. Seymore took the net from her and began working to get the albino bat into the cage. In the process, the bat bit him, but he held onto the magical creature until it was in the cage. Once inside, the bat covered its face and head with its wings.

The guide was covered in bats, spinning and screaming in his native language trying to get them off.

Now very unsteady, Alice grabbed onto Seymore. He took hold of her, as well as the caged albino bat, and began to make his way to the original entrance. There were multiple stops and starts, turning one way and retracing his steps, while trying to hold Alice up. She leaned against the wall, falling to her knees. Seymore tried to help her back to her feet. He then realized that Alice, like Dels, was infected with the virus. She was becoming dead weight. He began to panic, afraid of catching the virus and being stuck in the cave to die.

"Alice! Alice!" he yelled.

She was lost in a high fever and began to mutter. Seymore put the cage down next to her and cradled her head as he looked behind them, hoping for the guide to come and help.

"Feed me the albino bat," Alice said. "It will save me."

Seymore looked at the bat and slowly opened the cage. He needed to steel himself—*but against what? Fear? The virus? From all this madness?*

Carefully, he reached into the cage and took hold of the bat as Alice began to vomit violently and struggle to breathe. She began her death rattle, and then her face went motionless, eyes open, jaw still. She was dead. There was nothing he could do for her now. The albino bat surprised Seymore by biting his hand. It then flew out of the cage, attacking his face. Alice's words echoed in his head: "Feed me the bat; it will save me." In one furious motion, Seymore grabbed the bat and bit deep into its chest, ingesting its heart. He dropped to his knees and held his mouth closed to keep from spilling any of its blood. This was his salvation now, and he needed to eat it all. The albino bat shivered in his hands, then went still and silent.

Getting to his feet, Seymore started to make his way out of the cave until he was hit with seizures. He tried to fight through them, but they rolled through him violently like continuous earthquakes. The cave shook beneath his feet. He fell to the ground in a maddened state, rolling in pain, crawling. Hallucinating. The walls in the cave called his name. He twisted in pain, for how long he didn't know… *hours? Days?* He hoped and prayed to die. "Kill me already," he screamed.

Seymore felt his body being torn apart from the inside out like an intensely primal birth. He screamed in pain; his chest ripped open; his legs shriveled into his body. He reached for his chest but found his arms and hands were now wings.

He fully exploded, metamorphosing into the albino bat. He flew around chaotically, bouncing off walls before disappearing deep into the cave.

The room was dark. Seymore tried to sit, but his head was heavy. He was on a bed, maybe a cot. Still feeling confused, he found the floor with his feet, realizing his hearing was never this good, this clear. Seymore touched a small table with a lamp on it and turned on the light. The cot, table, and lamp were the only furniture in the room. There were no windows, nothing on the walls, and one small door. He could not remember anything but a vague memory of flying. Must have been a dream. Images of feeding on mice, rats, and maybe even a cat flashed before him.

He got to his feet and walked like a newborn fawn to the door. Outside the room was a long hallway; its walls were filled with art. A beautiful chair sat at the center of the blue foyer. It was a complete contrast to the dull room he had left. At the end of the hallway, there was a red door that he presumed led outdoors.

He opened the door. An older couple sat on the porch, surprised to see him. "You're up," the man said.

Seymore nodded his head.

"You've only been getting up at night," the man said.

"I don't mean to be rude, but who are you?"

"I'm Philip Philips. P. Philips. This is my wife, Victoria."

"Where am I?"

"Scotland."

Scotland? How the fuck did I get to Scotland?

JACK KELLY

Study time comes as it always does, but I cannot help myself. I look out the window of my classroom and expect to see Kasper Greenstreet standing with a cigarette in his hands, waiting for me.

Of course, he is not there. He never will be again. *Can a ghost that is presumably the soul of a dead person leave some dust? The spirit leaves a body behind, but are there remnants a ghost leaves behind?*

As hard as I tried to make the ghost of Kasper Greenstreet move on and leave Peter, his apartment, and the physical world, I miss him. *No. Maybe that is the wrong way to phrase it.* My feelings have been misplaced because I have spent the majority of eighth grade watching for him, waiting for him in the afternoon, and then looking for him in the spirit world. Now my days are haunted by the lack of his presence. The apartment is empty. It is a loss. I believe making his spirit move on was my mission, but now I wonder where he went and if there is anything his ghost left behind. *There is the painting...*

Looking at the apartment window, I write on my schoolbook cover: "Pull the shades down at Peter's! Add Kasper to *The Book of Souls*." *The Book of Souls* is a black notebook in which I write the names of people whom I am meant to care for spiritually. It all started with Katherine and my kids. Dr. Melvin, the psychiatrist I was seeing after my fall, insisted that my near-death experience created what he claimed was an imaginary family. He wanted me to stop thinking and talking about them. Get on with my life. Instead, I wrote their names in my notebook so I will never forget them. I refer to it as *The Book of Souls*.

I call Julia, Peter's mother, as soon as I get out of school. I've been working for Peter and his parents for most of the school year. They have become like family to me. She sounds troubled.

"Hello?"

"Julia, it's Jack."

"Jack, thank God you called. Can you come with me to see Peter? Something happened, but I'm not sure what."

Julia Cairo is waiting for me in front of her building, alone. We walk through Stuyvesant Town quietly and then up 1st Avenue to Bellevue Hospital. "I've tried calling, but I can't get any answers." She says breaking the silence.

It is more of the same when we arrive. Neither of us can visit him. Apparently, Peter had a violent outburst. Julia talks to the doctor like she is talking about a son my age, not a grown man. "My Peter hit someone?"

"Yes, I'm afraid he did."

"Well, why can't we see him?" I interrupt. "Maybe he needs us."

The doctor tilts his head like a dog. He is not the same doctor who let me in the last time. His face says *who are you?* "I'm his friend, Jack," I answer without being asked.

"Friend?"

"Yes," Julia says. "Jack is a friend of the family."

"Peter is very agitated," the doctor finally explains. "He is under the belief that some of the staff and patients are wicked—demonic—and that they are spying on him. Out to kill him is the way he phrased it."

Julia puts her hand to her face. "Oh, my God! My God! What is happening to my boy, Doctor?"

"It's still too early to diagnose, but he is showing signs of paranoid schizophrenia."

He is wrong, but I can't explain what has really happened: Kasper Greenstreet's ghost, the shadows, the haunting of apartment 3C. That should be Peter's diagnosis. But if I say it, they will lock us both up.

Julia and I don't speak as we walk back to her apartment. She does, however, hold my hand. She smells of ammonia which is the scent of her fear; of course, Julia smells fine to everyone else. It is just one of my abilities. I can smell some people's fear, anger, emotions. With others, I pick up their aura, their vibration. I can tap into all four of the known intuitions but, of course, not all the time.

There is clairsentience which is clear feeling—picking up the energy in the room. Claircognizant—clear knowing. Those are the moments when you know exactly how to choose. Even if rational reasoning is pointing to B, you know you must choose A. Clairaudience is clear hearing. This can be something as simple as having trouble with a decision and a song comes on the radio and the lyrics provide guidance. The last one, clairvoyance, is known as clear seeing. It can manifest as seeing pictures, images, or symbols. I have that with Peter's father, Mr. Cairo. He had a stroke and can't speak. When I first started working for him and Julia, I picked up symbols over his head. Julia was a red heart, Peter was a blue blanket, and I was a question mark.

We walk through the playground area of Stuyvesant Town. I can feel and perceive her old mental tapes running—Julia sitting on the bench while Peter plays as a little boy. I feel that she is remembering those were the happiest times of her life. The thought of that changes her smell to lemon Pledge.

"It will be all right, Julia," I finally say. "Peter's just going through a rough time."

She nods and puts her hands to her face. "Oh, my God, paranoid schizophrenia? Thank God for you," Julia says before walking into her building.

Afterward, I decide to visit Mr. David.

Mr. David greets me in a bathrobe and slippers, not ready for primetime. It is a far cry from the way he was dressed the first time I met him. He looked more like a businessman than a psychic. It was after my fall, and Aunt Paula took me to see him because of my near-death experience. Of course, we didn't tell my father. Mr. David became my mentor and introduced me to the mystics, who helped me understand my gifts. I have never seen him with one hair out of place—until today. *He is surprised to see me. Apprehensive may be more accurate. I'm here looking for guidance, but who is going to guide him?* Mr. David tells me about the mystic group's troubles. He also explains that he is unable to advise or give readings to any of his clients at this time.

"That day in the apartment has left us pretty fucked up." I've never heard Mr. David use the word "fuck," but honestly, it is a much better description than "in grave shape."

I brought Kasper Greenstreet to life for all of them. Now I feel responsible for their shift, for their lives being upended.

"He's gone," I say, like that will change everything back to the way it was.

Mr. David looks at me.

"He's gone. I made him leave," I say again, waiting for… *what?*

The mystics dabble in the paranormal, but to actually see and meet a ghost—a spirit—especially one as fierce and persistent as Kasper, is like viewing the Earth from the moon. It's not something you can just file away, nor is it what they really wanted. It's not a shape or an image on a photo. They are haunted by it, by shadows, by things that have negatively affected them. Their lives are turned upside down. *No. That's not what they wanted. Not at all.*

Mr. David sits. "How can you be sure?"

"Oh, I'm sure."

He does not ask for details, and I don't give them.

"Maybe we can all get back to normal," I say. "You know, the group?"

Mr. David looks at me. His words say "sure," but his look says something else entirely. Like with Kasper, it will never be as it was.

No one is home when I get to my apartment. Mail in hand, I hold the four envelopes that will decide the next four years of my life. *Should I wait for my dad before I open the letters?* I don't have that kind of patience. *Sorry, Mr. La Guardia, sorry, lion.* I start with my fourth-choice high school: Power Memorial. If my fourth choice accepts me, that typically means I've done pretty well on the test. I rip open the envelope. *Yes! I'm in!* That's a good sign. Next is Immaculata, my third-choice school; though deep down, this is the school I really want to attend. *Yes! Two for two!* Now comes La Salle. This is tricky because it's my number two. If I had never met Peter, it would have been my number one. It also happens to be a lot of kids' number one choice, so I hope I didn't blow it. They, too, have accepted me.

I look down at the last envelope—Xavier. I'll be proud of myself for getting in, but *do I really want to attend that school?* It's confusing. Quite frankly, it wasn't on my radar until I met Peter. Now it's Xavier, like I am following in his footsteps.

They have put me on the waiting list. Which is both good and bad. My scores are good enough for them to consider me, but it's a passive aggressive way to attend the school that I really want to attend. I can say, "I'm on Xavier's waiting list, but I'm not going to wait."

With Kasper Greenstreet gone, I expect Peter to get better immediately and come home to apartment 3C, his job—his life. But it doesn't work out that way.

Julia, Peter's dad, and I make our trek up 1st Avenue like nomads. I push Mr. Cairo in his wheelchair as the blue blanket representing Peter floats above his head. Julia is bundled up like it's freezing. It's the end of March, and it's going out like a lion. *As for me? I'm happy we are able to see Peter.*

Of course, we do a lot of waiting around. Patience is needed which seems to be the current theme in my life. This time, he wants to see Julia and Mr. Cairo first, which only seems right. While they are visiting, I raid the vending machine. Sitting in the waiting area of the psyche ward, I observe visitors and doctors to see if I pick anything up. *Still playing with fire, huh, Jack?* Then all hell breaks loose. An ambulance arrives with a woman losing her shit. I know this woman. *Jesus, it's the mad hatter from the incident on the subway!* She is screaming every obscenity I know and some I am hearing for the first time. She holds a woman's wig, which she fights fiercely to hold onto.

"Fuck you, demon!" she screams.

Is she looking at me? Kasper called me that. Demon. Only, this woman is calling everyone a demon, so I don't take it personally.

I'm out of sorts from all the screaming and "motherfucking demons!" the mad hatter throws around. Being so close to someone drowning in their mental illness makes me feel uneasy, unsure, and a little crazy by the time I finally get to see Peter.

I lean down to hug him. "No touching," the attendant says.

Peter is different today. Calm. More like Peter. "Tell me, did you get into Xavier?" he asks.

"How did you know I got my results?"

Peter smiles. *Yes! Peter is smiling! It's been a long time since I've seen him smile.* "They come the same time every year," he says.

"And you remember that?"

"Of course. It's such a big day."

"Waiting list," I say, embarrassed.

"They put you on the wait list?" He pauses, then nods. "I'll write a letter."

"No, that's okay. You've done so much for me already."

"Jack, it's a great school. Don't you want it?"

"Yeah." Which means *I don't know… maybe not.*

"Don't worry. I'm still a brilliant lawyer," he says with a wink.

"When you coming home?"

"Maybe this week."

"Great."

"I'm going to stay with my parents," he says.

"He's gone, Peter. The apartment is rid of him."

Peter's expression changes like the sky right before a storm. "It's only temporary." He stops making eye contact with me. "I think we are going to move to the Catskills for a few months. Get out of the city for a while."

Leaning in, I speak in a conspiratorial whisper. "Did you hear me? Kasper Greenstreet is gone." His name alone commands major emotions in Peter.

"I will never return to that apartment," he says firmly.

Silence. *Nothing is the same. Nothing. I thought I fixed everything.* Some things can't be fixed completely, like Peter and Mr. David's mystic group.

After a few beats, Peter looks at me again. "I was hoping you would help my mother sell or donate the furniture, dishes—I don't really care. Except for a very few personal items, everything else can go. My mother knows what I want to keep."

"Of course, I'll help."

"I'll pay you."

"Peter…" Now it's my turn to look away. *This all sucks. Time for me to go.*

As we get up from the chairs, Peter's smile returns. "This will be good for me, Jack—a new start. I will write an amazing recommendation letter for you. You will be an asset anywhere you go."

I want to say *it won't be good for me. Don't go! Don't move! Don't write a letter.* But "thanks, Peter" is all I can say.

While fighting back tears, I walk with a jubilant Julia back to their apartment. On the way, we run into my friend Brick. "Julia, Mr. Cairo, would you give me a minute? I want to say hello to a friend."

"Hey, I'm Brick. I saved this guy's life," Brick says, introducing himself in his usual grandiose fashion.

Julia doesn't know what to make of him, but she is happy about Peter coming home so nothing can spoil her mood.

I walk a few feet away with Brick before quietly asking, "Listen. Where are you going to be in twenty minutes? I need to get some weed."

After depositing the Cairos in front of their building, I politely refuse the offer to go up to the apartment. Julia and I set up a time to meet and plan the estate sale.

Brick is right where I asked him to be. I buy a dime bag; he lights up a joint rolled in hash oil. Everything's better when you are comfortably numb. The buzz saves me from dealing with my feelings, breaking down, and crying in the middle of 1st Avenue. *You can slay a dragon but you can't handle people leaving? I shake my head.* For the first time in a while, I think of Katherine and my kids, the happily married man I thought I was before I woke up in the hospital to learn I was a teenage boy with head injuries. The doctors who thought I would never walk again. All the physical therapy, the pain, the rope my father ran through the apartment and made me use, clinging to it to get myself to the bathroom. The nights I pissed myself trying. All the people who told me, "We're praying for you." Willing myself to a full physical recovery. Returning to school and hearing the parents and teachers whisper that my recovery was a miracle. My father constantly reiterating "Jack, it's a miracle that you are alive and walking like nothing ever happened."

Only, it didn't feel like a miracle. My first experience with the metaphysical in the subway. All the psychic happenings, picking up people's thoughts, emotions, fears. Seeing spirits and ghosts. The woman who kept throwing herself in front of the train over and over again like she did when she committed suicide. Realizing I could help her. The incredible migraines. The physically painful reminder for my foolish behavior… messing around in a condemned boarding house. Listening to Dr. Melvin insist that Katherine and the kids were imagined, a result of the insult to my brain created by the fall. The tears, my heartache trying to accept that… *I still don't—won't. Which makes me what? As crazy as Peter?*

Now, I want to remember them.

Think, Jack. What can you remember? What do you remember about Katherine? The kids? Think! The last time you saw them…

It is morning; I'm making breakfast... Something happened. A bird got in the house. No, that wasn't the last time. The phones in my office are ringing, exploding; Katherine is calling; one of the kids is sick; a bird hits the office window. No, that happened at school. I can't clear my head, my thoughts. *Remember, Jack. Remember...*

Tears run down my face. *What a mess. I seem to lose everyone.*

It's been a few days since we saw Peter. Now Julia and I are in his apartment getting ready to sell his things. I feel uncomfortable being alone with Julia in Peter's apartment. She has no idea what happened here, what really sent him to Bellevue: a suicide, a haunting, shadows. The strangeness created by a ghost that did not want to leave wreaked havoc on the living who encountered him. He derailed Peter's hope for a new life, his excitement for his girlfriend, for being back in the city he grew up in. Peter had a break-up, then a breakdown, and then almost killed me. I didn't and will never tell Julia how Peter chased me with a butcher knife while locked in the mental chains of madness. She knows nothing about my abilities. The memories I have are transcending—life altering—so it is painful to move on. *I feel hollow. I have no one to turn to—not Katherine, the kids, Peter, or the mystics. Not even Kasper waits for me anymore.*

"What is this?" Julia calls out.

When I walk into the guest bedroom, she is standing in front of the painting. "Oh. Yes, I found that in Peter's storage, left by a previous tenant." *I should have hidden it somewhere.*

"We should contact them. It's a strange painting." Julia says, looking it over. "Wait." She reads the name. "This is a Kasper Greenstreet?"

She knows of him, of his very large moment. "Yes, it is."

Julia looks at me. "It was in Peter's storage bin?"

"Yes."

"No one missed it?" It's a rhetorical question, so I don't answer. "Do you know who Kasper Greenstreet is?" She asks like she wants to educate me.

"...Yes."

"I should think it's worth some money!"

"Yes, I would say so."

Before we can continue, the intercom rings, letting us know potential buyers are here for the estate sale. Three women walk into the apartment. An older couple arrives moments later. They are from the building. Lookie-loos. I'm sure they've heard all the stories about the insanity in this apartment.

The intercom rings again. "Jack, do you think you can go downstairs and put something in the door, so we don't have the constant buzzing?" Julia asks.

When I return, a man is in the apartment. He looks familiar; I think I've seen him before. Something about him seems out of place; no, not out of place—out of time. Like he wandered into the wrong movie. He stands in the guest room, admiring the painting. More than that, he's communing with it, smelling it, touching it. *It's beyond peculiar. It is eerie.*

"That's not for sale!" I blurt out.

He turns to face me. *Yes, I know this guy.* "You are?" he asks in a voice so familiar that it's hypnotic. My mind and blood are racing.

"Jack," I answer.

"All work and no play make Jack a dull boy."

"Who says I don't play?"

"Touché," he says, walking over to me and reaching out to shake my hand. "Philips. I'm Mr. Philips," he says, but I hear *Philip.* "I would love to add this to my collection. I'm an admirer of the painter."

The man is unnerving. There is something very alarming about him. Danger. Evil itself? His hand is icy, then hot. My gifts and abilities alarm me. This is a hunter…

The feeling that someone has walked up behind me is reinforced by the smell of Julia's nervous energy. She distracts me, which makes me unhappy; I do not want to take my eyes and concentration off Philips. I must remember everything about him in detail.

"Nice to meet you, Mr. Philips," I say, "but as I said, it's not for sale."

He looks at me like he is reading me. Trance-like. Trying to figure something out.

Mr. Philips turns and walks back to the painting. He picks it up. *This guy has some fucking balls.* He stands with his back to us. Yet, I feel like he's watching me, which he is; I see his reflection in the bedroom window. His eyes are indeed on me. For a minute, I think he's going to climb out the window with the painting, which is ridiculous, but still, I feel as if he could. *He's so fucking creepy. Draculaesque.*

Turning his head toward me in a wicked manner, Mr. Philips smiles. If he wasn't so odd, you might say he's handsome, but his weirdness dispels that thought. "I can make you an indecent offer."

It is the way he says it that makes Julia gasp, but she says nothing.

I bet you can fucker. I say again, "It's not for sale."

The climate and mood in the room change drastically. It's dark and cold. I wait for him to shake the apartment in much the same way that Kasper Greenstreet did on the night I got him to leave. Only, he turns his back to us and faces the painting, wanting to be alone with it, as if he is trying to absorb the energy in the painting for himself.

I clear my throat. "Anything else?"

Mr. Philips puts the painting back where I had it, turns, walks over to me, and hands me a business card with only his name and telephone number. No address, no title. "If you change your mind—" *and you will* "—and decide to sell, call me." I know that he is speaking, but he is also sending me thoughts, telepathic commands.

Up until this point, he has not acknowledged Julia. Finally, he glances at her. She squeezes my arm. Philips returns his gaze to me and locks eyes with great intensity and power. *Wicked.*

"I've not seen a Kasper Greenstreet for sale in… forever." *You will give it to me!*

Fuck you, asshole; it's not for sale! But wait… that voice.

"As I said, I'm a big fan of Kasper Greenstreet."

I don't really hear his last name, but I know. *Yes, that's it—he is Philip. Now he calls himself Mr. Philips?*

Are you Philip? I want to ask because the anger that man created within Kasper Greenstreet's ghost was explosive. The shadows on the wall that night showed pictures of this man. The shadows let us hear his voice and Kasper's uncle's voice. *I can't and won't forget that moment.*

"Will you excuse me?" Mr. Philip says. *Before I tear off both your heads.*

Apparently, Julia and I are blocking the doorway of the bedroom. "Oh, yes, of course." Julia says, moving quickly. She is frightened but is unsure why.

I step out of the doorway very slowly, never taking my eyes off him. Julia and I exchange looks. We stick our heads out of the bedroom very carefully, watching as he exits the apartment.

"That was spine-chilling," Julia says.

"Yup. Let's get this painting put safely in the closet."

"Thank you, Jack. You handled that beautifully."

At the end of the day, the majority of furniture, dishes, and other goods have been spoken for. Julia is concerned about leaving such a highly valuable painting in the apartment unattended especially after the way Mr. Philips behaved when he saw it. *I don't blame her.* We discuss bringing it to her apartment; however, I'm sure Peter is not going to want anything belonging to Kasper Greenstreet in his parents' apartment. Not now, not when he gets out, not ever.

But Julia doesn't know that. "We should have that conversation with Peter," I say, "since ownership of the painting hasn't been established." Julia looks at me like *what are you, a fucking lawyer?* Maybe she just doesn't like me using "we;" though, a smile appears on her face.

"Good point, but still that painting has to be worth at least $25,000. I would think; although, to be honest, I have no idea," she says.

Take that and multiply by ten, Julia. Of course, I don't say it, afraid she may faint. This painting must possess something powerful within it. I remember reading the book about the countess returning it to Kasper because of its bad energy. *I was a witness to those shadows coming off the canvas! Philips is not just an admirer of the artist. There is something in that painting he needs.*

Rather than leaving it in the closet, we decide to find a better place to hide the painting without damaging it. I pick it up and do a double take. Kasper Greenstreet is still the child, but the shadows have returned. When I pause at the window to get a better look, it seems the painting is shifting back to the original version: a child with several sinister shadows surrounding it. *This shit just won't stop.*

"What is it?" Julia asks.

Not sure what or how much to tell her, I decide to keep my mouth shut. "It's nothing."

We hide the painting between Peter's mattress and box spring, about the only thing that has not sold. It brings us close in a conspiratorial way. Julia makes the bed to make it appear as natural as possible. "I'm sure it will be safe here," she says, proud of herself.

She refuses to let me walk her home. "Such a gentleman, your dad raised you right. But I'm fine, Jack. It's not even seven o'clock."

I leave her on the corner of 2nd Avenue. Every instinct and intuition in my body tells me to go back to Peter's apartment and remove the painting, which I do.

SEYMORE HUNTER

Seymore thought he had contracted the virus, which clouded his memory. *How did he get to Scotland?* He couldn't remember. His last clear memory was of traveling with Alice and Dels to Eastern Europe from London. He let the couple, the Philips, nurse him. *Who names their son Philip when his last name is Philips? Philip Philips? How ridiculous.* Physically, he felt very strong, actually stronger than he ever had. His hearing somehow had changed, too. Whispers sounded as loud as full conversations, even at some distance. He learned to control the intensity of sounds, so they didn't drive him crazy. He hoped all of his memory would come back to him eventually.

The couple told Seymore they had found him on the side of the road one morning like a wounded animal. He was confused, they said, talking about a cave. About friends now dead due to the virus spreading in Russia and Eastern Europe, Romania included. They were happy to inform him that the virus did not spread past those regions. Whatever caused its initial rampage had slowed and was no longer considered deadly, at least not in Scotland or England.

This information relaxed Seymore and helped trigger his memory, starting with the last day in the cave when he lost Dels and Alice to the virus… then finding an albino bat and eating its heart. *Why did he eat the heart? Why did he kill that beautiful creature in such a vicious manner? It was so confusing.* Slowly the memory of that trip filled in, like his other powers. He recalled dining with counts and countesses. Dabbling in the occult. Alice's reason for this trip: eating a bat's heart or liver while it was still breathing so she could remain young and powerful. Then he remembered Alice's last words: "Feed it to me. It will save me."

But they had not been looking for an albino bat; they had no knowledge of such a creature. It was folklore—an amazing find. *Did it now give him something more than extended youth?*

Whispers of Hitler, Germany, and war grew louder as Seymore's mind became as strong as his body. At night he walked, putting his newfound mystical and physical powers together. What he thought a dream due to the virus was, in fact, true. Seymore remembered his body painfully transforming into the albino bat. After struggling at first to fly, he was able to control its wings. Seymore possessed the albino bat's abilities and instincts but with a human brain. He began to experiment. If he killed or even bit another animal, he was able to take on those characteristics later. They had to be alive when he ate a piece of the heart or liver, though.

This began his education and life as a shapeshifter. Seymore spent his nights exploring the Scottish countryside, changing and learning how to use each shifting form for greater and greater use. He had to be careful approaching certain larger animals because of their physical power. When he learned that Philip Philips was a hunter, Seymore asked Philips to teach him to shoot and track an animal.

The man became a mentor in the art of tracking and killing animals for food. They started with ducks and worked their way to larger, more powerful animals, like boars and deer. There was much to learn, and Seymore became a skilled shot.

Knowing that the animals needed to be taken alive, Seymore began to venture out on his own, stray from Philips, or leave him behind completely. He practiced taking an animal down so it was injured and no longer a danger to him. At that point, he was able to eat its heart while it was still beating. This provided him with the ability to absorb and shape their DNA, to turn the animal's strength and prowess into his own mystical power.

The problem was that he had begun to enjoy the taste of blood and became interested in bigger, more powerful prey, like wolves and bears, which Philips wouldn't hunt. Seymore tried hard to leave Philips at night in order to get to animals one wouldn't serve on a dinner table. One night, he slid out from their private camp as Philips lay sleeping. But Philips had become suspicious after Seymore disappeared the last two times they hunted. Philips thought he heard animal sounds outside the house in the middle of night but only found Seymore returning from one of his many nocturnal walks.

Hearing Seymore leave the tent, Philips waited to see if he had stepped out for a piss. When he didn't return, Philips decided to track him, taking a gun and a flashlight. Philips had seen great growth in Seymore's hunting skills, and his eagerness to learn at first was exciting. But now it was suspicious. Outside the tent, he tracked Seymore's footprints into the woods. He followed his boot tracks deep into the hillside until they came to a stop. Philips shined the light on the ground, spotting footprints a good six feet ahead. *Baffling.* It took Philips multiple starts and stops until he found Seymore's boots and clothes neatly folded and hidden in bushes. *Why on earth would he undress?* Philips took a piece of toilet paper from his pocket and wrapped it on the branch where the clothes and boots were placed. Then he began tracking Seymore's bare footprints, which started a good six feet from where the last boot print was noted. *Did he jump?* Within twenty feet, all of the prints disappeared. This astonished Philips, who began spinning in place. He looked up at the rocks for some sign of Seymore. There was nothing to track; it was as if he flew away.

The sound of a gunshot rang in the far distance. Philips kept climbing toward the top of the ridge. He could hear the sounds of wolves in distress and cautiously moved toward that direction. Within minutes, a pack of wolves moved past him. They were not hunting but appeared to be the prey, which was not possible in the area.

The silence that followed made Philips pause. His heart pounded so loudly in his chest he did not hear a wounded animal in distress or of another animal feeding. Philips stumbled upon Seymore, now bizarrely large, eating the heart of a wolf who was still alive. Philips froze in shock, fear, and disgust until it was too late. The creature stood and smashed Philips to the cold ground, breaking his neck. Seymore took his first taste of a human heart and then assumed Philips' identity as well.

The hunting accident left Philip Philips unidentifiable. By the time Seymore returned to fully human form and led authorities to his friend's body, a multitude of wild animals had fed on it.

Afterward, Seymore stayed with the widow. He began going out into the countryside at night to practice his shapeshifting. He had already killed a menagerie of animals and a human; now, he began to play with the mix. Who would dare fight with a creature that was part wolf and part bear, with the hearing of a rare albino bat and the reasoning power of a human?

All of his memories came back to him while he practiced shapeshifting: how he met Dels at a men's upscale clothing store. His affair with Alice. The scams Alice and Dels perpetrated on people, and the love they all shared for the occult. After learning as much as he could in the countryside, Seymore told the widow he was moving on, using the loss of his great friend and mentor Philip Philips as the reason. He wanted to get back to London to use his new power to make money and prepare for his trip to America.

London had not changed much since his time away. With his newfound abilities, Seymore was able to get in and out of flats and stores, stealing money and anything else he could sell on the black market. His physical appearance, fashion sense, and powers enabled him to collect people that enriched his pockets, as well as his other appetites. The louder the talk of war, the more eager Seymore was to escape to America. His abilities provided him wealth but also created a thirst for more. More violence, more trouble, more wanting to live longer. Perhaps forever.

Seymore also found he couldn't stay away from people who bargained with the Devil—sorcerers, witches, necromancers, spiritualists, mediums, and occultists. He explored all their gifts and powers while never revealing his own. He settled on the necromancer, a being that can live inside and outside of death. Necromancers also have the abilities to communicate with and utilize entities such as ghosts, shadows, and misguided spirits. This became another of his skills, his powers.

Now Seymore had the ability to steal, misappropriate antiquities, and even kill without ever being caught. However, people he swindled began suspecting him of a multitude of sins as did the authorities. Shapeshifting began to change his look slightly over time, presenting him as a man in the wrong picture, the wrong movie, the wrong place.

Seymore was searching for what happened to the painting in Alice Walker's entry, the one with the shadow. He met a sorcerer who was convinced it was an entity you could use for power and possibly a longer life. Seymore remembered Alice stating the same thing about the painting, that she used it to uncover people's secrets, fears, and inner demons. He discovered that the painting had been sent to her family in America once her body was recovered from the cave and the estate settled.

As he planned to leave for America, one item sat on Seymore's mind: Alice Walker's mysterious and possibly powerful painting. His mission was to find the painting with the nefarious shadow. At the start of the summer of 1939, before the war in Europe began, he crossed the *Queen Mary* as one of its last passengers. Three months later, the ship was retrofitted as a troop ship and renamed the *Grey Ghost.*

Seymore had big plans to explore America with all its possibilities. The painting would give him a perfect arsenal of power.

He searched for the better part of two decades but never saw Alice Walker's painting again. He did eventually find documentation—an insurance claim—provided by one of her nieces. The artwork had been destroyed in a fire in 1946.

SEYMORE HUNTER MEETS KASPER GREENSTREET

The *Duality* exhibit of a little-known artist by the name of Kasper Greenstreet was not on Seymore Hunter's radar, alias P. Philips, when a rich female patron of the arts invited him to a showing at the Guggenheim. Philips stood behind a long line of people enamored by the two paintings of the actress Desiree Diamond, who had died earlier that day. Philips could smell the blood; he knew the artist was using it in his work. *Many of the paintings had a mystical look but did any hold real power? Real magic?*

That's when his body began to pulsate. In an area with fewer people, Philips beheld the most amazing painting he had ever seen: the self-portrait of the artist as a child surrounded by three shadows. He moved everyone out of his way and moved close enough to smell it, taste it. Philips felt the energy coming from the painting and knew he had to possess it at any cost. He wanted to be legitimate so he offered every dime he had accumulated or robbed in the bidding process, only to be told he had been outbid. The painting had been sold to some countess.

He knew other ways of getting the painting. Viler, more sinister ways. Before he had a chance, the countess naively returned it to Kasper Greenstreet, overwhelmed by the mystical, dark side of the art without an ability to control its hidden wickedness. Then Philips began following Kasper Greenstreet. He needed to taste his blood, maybe eat his heart. Kasper slipped through his hands due to an interruption by a couple of drug addicts whose bodies were found weeks later. Accidental overdose. The taste of Kasper's blood would always keep him on Philips' radar.

Then Kasper Greenstreet did the unimaginable. He committed suicide. He left the painting and all its power in the hands of some teenage kid and a psychologically damaged adult. None of it mattered now. The painting was close to being his. He could feel it. Young Jack Kelly had powers, but in the end, his power would be no match for Seymore Hunter, aka Philip Philips.

JACK KELLY

School is boring. I've gone from fighting and seeking to understand shadows, demons, and ghosts to trying to figure out what X equals.

I'm no longer able to leave the classroom, even if my head is exploding. These are the terms and conditions we signed off on. No more special treatment for me. I got into more trouble for missing my appointment with Father Keenan than I did for missing two days of school for being sick.

I give Sister Elizabeth nothing to write in her journal today. I'm on my best behavior. At 1:50 p.m., I grab my books, walk to her desk, and politely ask her if I may be excused to see Father Keenan. He works in the uptown offices of the archdiocese. However, his agreement with Sister Thaddeus and my father is for him to come to the Epiphany rectory on 21st Street.

He does not keep me waiting. "Monsignor has been kind enough to let us use his office," he says.

I follow him to the office and take note of the place. It's my first time there. A large mahogany desk occupies the space, with two leather chairs directly in front of it and a smaller couch against the wall. There is a large bookshelf, pictures of the pope and other prominent people, a cross, and a painting of the Blessed Mother on the opposite wall.

Father Keenan sits at the desk and motions for me to sit in one of the chairs. I want to say *shouldn't I lay on the couch? But why cause trouble?*

"Would you like a glass of water?" Father Keenan asks.

"No, thank you."

"Do you know why you are here?"

"Sort of. You are concerned with some of my friends..."

He leans in. "Now why does a thirteen-year-old…"—"Fourteen," I interrupt—"…fourteen-year-old boy refer to adults in their thirties as 'friends?' Do you have friends your own age?"

"Well, because they helped me at a time when I needed people to care. And yes, I do have friends my age."

"Fair enough." He pours himself a glass of water. "Let me know if you change your mind about the water." Father Keenan locks eyes with me. "Do you know what the occult is?"

"Father, I don't practice black magic or witchcraft, if that's what you are asking me."

He nods. "Do you know what it is?"

"I do."

"Does this Mr. David, a known psychic, ever read you?"

"No."

"So, you understand what I mean by 'read you?'" Nodding my head is not the answer he wants. "What does it mean?"

I'm not going to play these bullshit games. I don't give a shit what Father Keenan and the others think about Mr. David. I'm not giving up his friendship or his advice. It may be a moot point now that they are all distancing themselves from me. My head is throbbing. I could use one of Brick's magic cigarettes now.

"Do you believe that séances, Tarot cards, and Ouija boards can open the door to another realm, to demons?" Father Keenan asks.

"No."

"Can you expand on your answer?"

"No, I don't believe that they can open the door. However, I've never been to a séance, played with Tarot cards, a Ouija board, or any of that shit."

Father Keenan does not seem offended by the word. "You like to curse, don't you, Jack?"

That I will cop to. "Yes, as a matter of fact, I do."

"Does it make you feel older—like less of a boy?"

"What does that mean?"

"Do your older friends curse around you?"

"Listen, after my fall, the doctor told my dad it was not unusual for patients with head trauma to curse. It's a bad habit, I admit, but I like it. It is a vice of mine."

"Do you have any other vices?"

"Father Keenan, what exactly are you and Sister Elizabeth afraid of? Do you think I practice witchcraft? I guess in the old days you could get away with a good old-fashioned witch hunt! Drown me! Burn me at the stake!" I deliberately do not say, *fucking drown me.*

Father Keenan puts his hands up. "Calm down, Jack. No one is accusing you of being a witch. At least not me."

We sit in silence, before Father Keenan asks if I have any questions for him. There are many, but I am only willing to ask one: "As Catholics, what is our belief in ghosts?"

He puts his two index fingers to his lips. "Like every religion, we Catholics are made up of a variety of people with different experiences. We do believe in the Trinity and, initially, the Holy Spirit was referred to as the Holy Ghost. Purgatory is the cleansing of a spirit where many spirits and ghosts reside. If we look at it that way, then yes, there is at least an acknowledgement of ghosts. It gets tricky when you bring black magic into it with the belief you can bring back Napoleon or Cleopatra through a séance or a channeler who claims to communicate with such spirits. You have to be careful with the word 'medium'—'psychic.' That is not meant as a jab."

"No jab taken," I say.

"Is there something personal behind your question?"

I shake my head. "Just curious."

My visit leaves me conflicted. *Did Kasper miss the opportunity to go to purgatory for a cleansing? Can I consider what happened between the two of us a cleansing? I wish I could visit that nun again. She—or her spirit—saved me from the shadows and the demons when I fell through the floor in the boarding house. She taught me how to fight them and go back to my body so I didn't die there. She is a spiritual guide for me; only, I don't know how to get back there.*

THE FADING MYSTICS

Mr. David and his group no longer meet. There is no yoga nor meditation sessions. Instead, he plans a meet-up for tea and coffee at our little bohemian coffee shop. I'm sure after the birds crashed into our school, Mrs. Dowd no longer comes here for coffee. She never makes eye contact with me at school anymore, either. It's not likely I will run into her today.

Mr. David has secured a table for us. He is the only one there when I arrive. "I'm not sure Raphael is coming," Mr. David says. "He has gone through a lot of changes."

Mr. David asked me one question on the phone before setting up this group meetup: "Is he still gone?" Then he never mentioned Kasper Greenstreet again. Nor have I.

To our surprise, Raphael is the first to arrive. He tries to put on a carefree face because that is who he typically was; only, it doesn't fit. Raphael is strained, uncomfortable. Susie comes in and orders a tea, then smells its aroma. "It is wonderful to be able to smell again," she says.

We remain silent, waiting for Star; it is an awkward silence. She is the last to arrive. Star acts the same as ever. Everyone is polite and seems very happy to see me. They talk about my next challenge: which high school I will go to.

"Graduation is getting close, Jack," Susie says. "You should be so proud of yourself."

"How is your tea, Jack?" Star asks.

"It's Earl Grey. You want a taste?"

"No, I'm good with the chamomile."

Normally, we would be in deep metaphorical and metaphysical conversation already. Or talking about our group meditation or how powerful the energy is in the circle. Everything has changed. The easy camaraderie is not here, at least not today. *The elephant in the room is sucking out all the air. That elephant is no longer a ghost. It is us.* Kasper Greenstreet is the name we dare not speak, so I never get around to telling them about the final night I had with Kasper. I can't tell them about the painting or Mr. Philips. Mr. David says he will not be doing the yoga and meditation groups, at least for a while. Raphael will be going on a retreat with his church. Star and Susie never mention Tarot, or readings. *It's just all bullshit, really.*

They don't ask about Peter and Bellevue Hospital, either. It is like we are strangers.

Walking home, I am lonely. I love that group. But as Mr. David said to me in private: "Things change. People change. Life doesn't stay the same, and if it did, you would be looking to change it. You are young. Your entire life is in front of you. There will be amazing things to come."

The emptiness I feel is wide and deep. "This too will pass," Mr. David says, his last words to me at the coffee house. I hope this passes quickly because I am uncomfortable with all these emotions.

I resent having to see Father Keenan but I do anyway. I have made commitments to my father, to myself, and to my school. I'm engaging in less lying and am trying to see all perspectives. *Guess it's not really over for Sister Elizabeth and the school since they really didn't know about Kasper Greenstreet and why I was so obsessed with apartment 3C.* Sister Elizabeth's breasts are back on my mind, but something has changed. Watching her from the corner of my eye, I am sure of it.

Father Keenan keeps me waiting. I'm always curious about what he will want to discuss. When he arrives, he ushers me into the office, asking questions. "So, you got your results from the Regents. How did you do?"

"Good."

"Which schools did you apply for?"

"La Salle Academy, Immaculata, Power Memorial, and Xavier."

"I went to La Salle. Why Immaculata?"

"Because it's co-ed."

"Why Xavier? It's one of the more difficult schools to get into. Very expensive."

"Well, Peter Cairo went there; he thought I should try."

"Hmm. Peter Cairo. Shame what's been going on in his life."

Uh oh. Did I just step in it?

When he sees the reaction on my face, Father Keenan doesn't miss a beat. "Can you define your relationship with Peter for me?" *Why is it I'm not afraid of shadows and ghosts, but his questioning terrifies me? I always feel like he wants to trap me.*

"Define?"

"Yes. You are a young man. We heard about the incident in his apartment."

"Incident?" I'm about to plead the fifth.

Father Keenan grows quiet. He looks at me and the papers on his deck, then back at me. *Remember. Patience, Jack. It's a card game.* Father Keenan continues moving papers around like he has all my information right in front of him.

"Yes, the police were called to his apartment. He was chasing you with a knife."

Here I go—time for Pinocchio. I'm about to start lying my ass off. "Knife?"

Father Keenan sits back in his chair. He picks up a paper. "Sister Elizabeth saw you being chased by Peter Cairo from your classroom window. He had a knife. She was one of the people who called the police. The police report said a knife was found at the scene. Two neighbors said they heard you yelling for help."

"No. No. No. I told the police officer that, um, I thought Peter was going to hurt himself." Father Keenan stares at me like the liar I am. He looks again at the paper in front of him, apparently the police report.

"Why were you in an adult male's apartment in the middle of the day? A dangerous adult male? Why would your father let you go there?"

"I work for the Cairos. Peter would never hurt me, not in his right mind..."

"But he's not in his right mind, is he? Isn't that the reason he's in Bellevue's psych ward?" Silence. Then, "Has Peter Cairo ever tried to touch you?"

This is ridiculous. "What?"

"Has Peter Cairo ever touched you?"

"Touched me?"

"Has he ever touched you inappropriately? Told you he loves you?" The buzzing in my head amplifies. "It's okay to tell someone if he asked anything improper of you," Father Keenan adds, thinking he is protecting me.

"Never. Never."

I am offended, but it's just a few months until I graduate, as my dad and Aunt Paula say. If I actually tell the truth, Father Keenan will think I'm nuts. It's easier for him to believe I may have been molested than buying into a ghost story. Or, in this case, a haunting in apartment 3C that caused Peter's breakdown.

"Father, do you have some Tylenol? I'm getting a massive headache."

Father Keenan stands immediately. "Yes, of course. Let me get you some."

While he is out of the room, I look at the police report, which is actually not a police report at all. That's not to say Father Keenan never saw it. He has a lot of connections in this city, and there are police officers and detectives among the parishioners.

When he comes back in the room, I take the Tylenol. It is the one thing I am not lying about. My head feels like it's about to explode.

The session ends, leaving me feeling dirty, confused.

DEMONS BY ANOTHER NAME

Peter is released from Bellevue while I'm at school. He promptly throws a shit fit when Julia talks about bringing the painting to the apartment; my instincts were correct. So much so that Julia surprises me by waiting on the corner for me after school.

"Julia?"

She motions for me to walk with her, aware that we are under the glaring eye of teachers and parents. Julia is sensitive to the stain that the "incident," as Father Keenan called it, has put on the Cairo name; only, she thinks it was a suicide attempt. Not to mention the additional stigma due to Peter's stay in Bellevue. We cross 2nd Avenue, heading east on 22nd Street. "Can you come to my apartment? Peter is home," she says.

"That's great, Julia!" I'm ecstatic about Peter's release.

"You were right; just the mention of bringing the painting to the apartment caused him to act like a lunatic." She pauses, looking to the ground, then up at me. "Sorry, that is a bad choice of words." We walk silently, like spies in the Cold War looking suspiciously at anyone close enough to pick up our conversation. "What's the matter with him? How can a painting he's never seen before make him so crazy?" *Another poor choice of words.*

"Peter just wants to put all this behind him. Anything that reminds him of that apartment. Maybe it has nothing to do with the painting," I lie.

When we get to the apartment, Peter is busy getting his dad situated on the couch after helping him take a shower. "He doesn't need a shower every day, Peter," Julia says.

"He wanted one," Peter says tersely.

It reminds me of one of my father's sayings: "The house is on fire, let's not worry about the dishes in the sink." But I don't say that to Julia. Instead, I whisper, "It's good for Peter to be busy."

I try to change the subject quickly. "Peter! It's so good to see you."

When he is happy with Mr. Cairo's positioning, he turns to me. He smiles, shakes my hand. "Let's go for a walk," he says.

Julia steps forward but immediately changes her direction and heads into the kitchen. "Okay. Enjoy." Her delivery is shaky, not believable.

We descend the staircase to the street. While on the staircase, there is a moment when I wonder if he's going to attack me. *Leftover dust?* Once outside the building, he sort of becomes the Peter I once knew. Smiling at me, he says, "Jack, you have no idea how happy I am to see you outside of that place."

"I feel the same way, Peter."

"I feel like I am waking up from a nightmare." A long pause follows, then he says, "Tell me about the painting."

"You remember I asked you about getting into the storage?"

"Yes."

"Well, I found a Kasper Greenstreet original inside. It was part of the *Duality* series. A self-portrait of him as a kid."

I don't tell Peter the original portrait had me as the kid. I've told no one. That secret will stay with Kasper Greenstreet and me, and Kasper is gone, in the afterlife. I honestly don't think Peter could recover if he knew I was the subject in the painting. I believe that is the reason Kasper and I came together, why I could see him, and why we found one another. That was also why I was the one able to release him from being trapped, earthbound.

Peter looks at me, surprised. "How do you know all this?"

"Well, I knew if I was ever going to get him out of your apartment, I needed to know everything I could about him. So, I spent all day at the main library studying his work and him. All of it was fascinating." He looks at me questioningly, wanting more. "What I found out helped me banish him from your apartment."

We walk a block in silence before he speaks. "How can you be sure he's really gone?"

"Oh, I'm sure. Trust me on that. It was the way he left."

We proceed along the East River. "My mother is being ridiculous, wanting to hang the painting up."

"Peter, she has no idea about what has happened; only we do." After a beat, I ask, "What are you going to do with the painting?"

"Find the owner. The provenance of the painting."

"What does that mean?"

"Well, the reason for provenance is to find out many things. Is it a forgery?"

"Definitely not," I say.

"Well, it needs to be proven. It's important to know if it is a fake, or if it was stolen, looted. Who the original owner was… did they sell it? Is there a chain of ownership? Because if you do that and prove it's true, it makes a big difference in its market value and who it belongs to now."

"Did your mother tell you about Mr. Philips?" I ask.

"Who is that?"

"When we were having the estate sale, a man—a Mr. Philips—came in and wanted to buy it."

"No. She said nothing of that. Where was the painting?"

"I left it out in the open, in the guest bedroom. It was my fault."

We become ourselves again. Peter, the smart lawyer taking an interest in educating me, the little brother—maybe the son—he never had. "I have his card…"

"But?"

I'm hesitant. *Peter just got out of Bellevue. Do I really want to drop Mr. Philips and his scary vibe on him?*

"Peter, when I was doing research, there was a book that the librarian referred to as 'sensationalism.' It said a countess bought the painting for more than $250,000 at the original offering."

Peter is shocked. "What?"

"Yes, but she returned it to the artist and the gallery because it had 'bad energy.'"

Peter looks at me, wanting to be done with Kasper Greenstreet, Mr. Philips, and the painting.

"I don't know if I should tell you this..." I say.

"Jack, I'm good. Seriously. I need to know this shit, even if I never look at the painting or return to the apartment again."

"Well, this book... it said the woman went mad. However, Kasper Greenstreet took the painting back through his gallery representative. I found it in your apartment's storage bin, which at one time was the apartment of Susan and Mitch Michaels, who owned the gallery." Peter's wheels are turning, making me a little anxious. "I'm sure I told you about the Michaels."

"Yes, you told me about them."

"Honestly, I think it was the painting that kept him attached to the apartment, to the building. Not the Michaels." More silence.

We watch the boat traffic on the East River. "Two hundred and fifty thousand dollars... that's crazy!" Peter says.

"Yeah, well that was in 1972. Who knows what it will sell for now? Seven years later."

Peter looks at me intently. "Tell me about the man in the apartment."

"Mr. Philips? He was salivating at the chance of being able to purchase it, but there is something wrong there. He was beyond strange. Very dark. Something..." I stop myself; not sure how fragile Peter still is.

"What are you saying, Jack?"

What AM I saying? The painting seems to have a life of its own. It was the tool that made Kasper move on, the tool that drove him to suicide. I'm not going to go into details; Peter doesn't need to know about the shadows coming out of the painting and attaching to the walls. But he does need to know that there were shadows in the painting itself. This makes him go quiet for a long time.

"Sounds like we shouldn't even think about selling it," Peter says. "I mean if it has some kind of negative—I don't know—power or energy... Do you?"

"No."

"And this Philips? What do you think he wants?"

"I don't think he's an art collector."

Peter goes quiet on me, and I let him. We walk for a long time before finding ourselves back in front of his parent's apartment building. "Oh, I wrote a really great letter to Xavier. Contacted my friend on the board," he says, breaking the silence.

When we go inside, Julia is glum. Her smell is all over the place, the scent of ammonia, body odor. Mr. Cairo has all kinds of things swirling over his head, a full windstorm. I pick up on their dispositions immediately; though, it takes Peter a minute.

"What's wrong, Mom?" he finally asks.

Julia takes a deep breath. "Someone broke into your apartment."

"When?"

"Late last night. They said it looked like a wild animal was let loose, tore the place up." Julia looks at me. "It appears they were looking for something."

"The painting?" Peter asks.

Julia shakes her head. "Gone."

I stop both of them. "No. It's not gone. I have it. After I left you on Sunday, Julia, I went back and took it. I didn't trust that Philips guy."

Julia knows the Kasper Greenstreet painting should be worth some money. Peter understands there is something sinister about the painting. I think it is worth a lot, but it's the shadows that make it priceless to anyone with evil intentions.

Just as I am about to register for Immaculata, my acceptance letter from Xavier arrives. I'm off the waiting list and on to "Thank you for choosing Xavier. You will be a member of the graduating class of 1983." It seems like a lifetime away. In my bones, I know this is a mistake. I should attend Immaculata, which is really more my speed, but how do you turn down the opportunity to go to Xavier? That's what I keep hearing from Dad, Peter, and everybody else.

Peter does his due diligence in regard to the painting. He refuses to pursue the break-in. The goal at hand is to find out what happened to the estate of Kasper Greenstreet. He wants to make sure that the book's account is true— that the countess returned the picture through legal means, making it Kasper Greenstreet's. He is also looking into the estate of Susan and Mitch Michaels, which may enable us to find the current ownership. According to court records, Kasper's estate has not been settled. The state of New York is still looking for heirs. Also, the numbers are a mess—the accounting does not reflect many assets or much money. *How does an artist who was that famous, selling art for big sticker prices, not have any money?*

Since Kasper did not have a spouse, children, or living parents when he died, it looks like the state of New York will take whatever assets he has unless they find a first cousin or a hidden will. The painting is not noted in the court records. However, the Michaels estate is different. Their wealth was divided between Susan's mother, a nephew, and two of Mitch's nieces. None of that matters to us; we are only after information concerning this painting. Original pictures of the painting will also be massively helpful; however, in all the library books, I only saw one. Peter hires a private investigator, Mr. Cohen, to help locate the relatives.

While all this is going on, Peter and his parents are planning to move out of New York and into a little town along the Hudson River where they can start over. Peter has a little money, as do his parents. I am at the end of my Epiphany career, which after eight years leaves me with mixed emotions. What started out as a miracle—me returning to school after the accident—has dwindled to *thank God we got through the eighth grade!* Several of my classmates think I'm a freak and rightly so. Looking at Sister Elizabeth, I see a running image of the chaos I created. Actually, that is not accurate; I do not believe I created the man dying on the train, nor did I create the demons, shadows, or birds crashing into our classroom windows. However, I must take ownership of my part in it. If I had never returned to school, none of it would have happened.

Sister Elizabeth and I tolerate each other; though, tolerate is probably the wrong word. I don't have any animosity toward her per se. She is one of the first people about whom I felt a strong premonition. The three breasts and all—of course, I have never seen them myself. But still, I feel strongly that I am accurate in that impression. While watching her from my desk, I do not believe my mission was simply to know that she had three breasts. Something else was at play. However, the events of the school year sidetracked me in my understanding. *I must ask the Holy Spirit for guidance, meditate, use all of my intuition and abilities. If there is something that I was or am supposed to know or do, it will be a shame if I do not at least try.*

Meanwhile, smoking pot seems to be relaxing me to the point where the voices and premonitions have quieted down. Graduation cannot come quickly enough, but before it does, I know that saying goodbye to Peter Cairo and his mom and dad will be by far one of the hardest things I will ever do.

Before it happens, Peter and I meet with the detective. I am Peter's right-hand man, his liaison to a painting he still has not seen. At the present moment, the painting is comfortably sandwiched between the mattress and box spring in Aunt Paula's and Uncle Willy's apartment. Our detective is an interesting man, ex-NYPD. *He wants to know why I am here but is reluctant to come right out and ask.*

Finally, he does. "No offense, but what's with the kid?"

"This is Jack," Peter says. "Everything I know, Jack knows. He actually knows more about the painting and Kasper Greenstreet than I do. I trust him with my life."

Detective Cohen nods but doesn't like it. Peter begins to take us through court documents on the two estates. The Michaels estate is settled. Susan's mother received the bulk of their wealth, plus papers, personal effects, and other items. However, she has passed away, leaving her estate to a cousin. Kasper's estate planning was messy. At the time of his death, he had just hired a new lawyer and accountant. The state of New York is looking for distant heirs, as well as assets. *Like old artwork sitting around?*

The name of a Candace Kunning comes up, but it appears to be an alias—one of numerous aliases the woman in question used. She was working at the gallery for Susan and Mitch at the time of their death. Apparently, she is a person of interest as she was the last one with access to gallery records. Peter and I will meet next with Kasper's lawyer and accountant. The fact that he includes me in all of this is blowing me away. The detective is here to find the cousin, nephews, nieces, and Candace.

Before we end the meeting, Detective Cohen has an announcement. "Full disclosure," he says. "I worked for Kasper Greenstreet very briefly before he died.

It catches us completely off guard. And I know there are no coincidences. "In what capacity?" Peter asks.

"Typically, I don't divulge my clients or their cases."

Peter, ever the lawyer, is not satisfied. "Well, I need to know if there is a conflict of interest. Besides, your client is dead."

The detective is silent. He weighs the difference between an old case with no money and a new case with money. Money wins. "He hired me to find somebody."

"A relative?" I ask. He shakes his head.

"A friend?" Peter asks.

"No."

My instincts and intuition push me. "Is his last name Philips?"

Cohen's body language and facial expression tell me I have hit his battleship. *Got him.* Peter takes out the business card with Mr. Philips' name on it and hands it to the detective. I've got a copy of the name and number at home.

"Well, yes and no," Detective Cohen says. "Interestingly Kasper only had his first name—Philip, not Philips. Which may have been one of the reasons I couldn't locate him. Although, this could just be a coincidence."

I don't think so, I want to say but stay quiet. "Can you tell us why he had you looking for him? Since we are on the same team now," Peter says.

Detective Cohen looks conflicted. On the one hand, he sits with new clients who prefer him to be tight-lipped about our situation. On the other hand, he wants our trust. His previous client, after all, is dead, and the dead don't talk—at least not anymore. After a certain amount of posturing, Cohen speaks. "My understanding is—was—that this man, Philip, attacked him."

"On the street?" Peter asks.

"You have to understand, Mr. Cairo, Kasper Greenstreet was very cagey about it all. So, he held back details, but I think it was a pick-up that went wrong. This Philip fucked him up pretty good. Really spooked him."

Yes, I did pick this up when the shadows revealed Kasper's fears. Philip made Kasper very irate, fearful, confused, and angry.

Looking at the business card, Cohen states the obvious. "Just a number. No address. How did you come by this Mr. Philips?"

Now it's my turn to be cagey, but Peter chooses full disclosure. "Jack and my mother were handling the sale of all my personal property in the apartment. This guy showed up. He told Jack he wanted to buy the painting," he says.

"Did you advertise the painting?" the detective asks.

"No. Of course not. That's why we're here—to find out the provenance of the painting."

"Maybe we should set up a meeting with this Mr. Philips," Mr. Cohen says.

"Not sure that's a good idea, until we secure provenance," I say.

The detective watches me very carefully. "How old are you?" he asks, clearly not a fan.

"Fourteen."

He looks at me, then at Peter. "Jack is as smart as they come. Plus, he has three balls." Our detective looks at us questioningly.

"Peter's just kidding about the smart part," I say. *No one has ever accused me of having three balls; I like it!*

We leave our detective to find the relatives. We will save Mr. Philips for another day.

TURN THE PAGE

I'm struggling with everything: the Cairos' planned move, graduation, my commitment to Xavier, and not seeing Mr. David or the mystics. Old habits die hard. Every day at the same time, I look for Kasper Greenstreet at the window of Peter's apartment. It makes no sense; that part is over. Yet, he lives on in my psyche as I search for records of the painting that brought us together. Peter has rented storage space for the painting. In the meantime, it remains in my Aunt Paula's apartment. Detective Cohen has found Mitch Michaels' two nieces and the nephew fairly easily. Susan Michaels' cousin is somewhere in Brooklyn. It's just a matter of time before he locates her, too.

Uncle Willy brings the painting back to apartment 3C. Peter will not come to the apartment nor look at the painting, which is baffling to me. *Face your fears!* Although that's easier for me to say, since I did not end up in Bellevue's psych ward. Julia and I will pack the painting while Peter makes the arrangements to have it moved with the help of the detective so our expensive piece of art makes it there in one piece. Peter has given us hand-written instructions on how to properly wrap the artwork. Julia and I work well together. She asks in a roundabout way if the Cairos have ever been the topic of conversation in the Parish. "No," I say quickly, not wanting to open that can of worms. Julia doesn't know that they monitor me. She does not know of my required visits with Father Keenan, that Sister Elizabeth does not think highly of me or her son, or that none of them are impressed with my "gifts."

I'm in the end game with apartment 3C and meeting with Father Keenan. My radar regarding Sister Elizabeth tells me there is unfinished business. Not in a bad way but still unfinished. There is something still to be worked out and discovered. A mustard yellow with outer rings of gray radiates around Sister, not from her skin, but her aura. The mystics taught me all about auras, their significance, and what colors represent a person's field of energy. Mr. David also told me to interpret the colors and to use my intuition. "Jack," he said, "you don't need a color chart. If it's telling you something, listen." Most days when I wake up and think about all this shit, I wish it were over. Before meeting with Father Keenan for the last time, I smoke a joint to calm my anxiety.

"Jack. I hear you were accepted to Xavier," Father Keenan says.

I nod. "Yes." *Not sure how he came by this information.*

"That's great news."

He quickly focuses the session on how proud he is of me for turning the ship around. No more talk of witches, spells, who I pray to, or if Peter Cairo is canoodling me. *I don't know what that means because I'm still out here in the water, with new battles to be fought.* He continues the pleasant conversation through questions: What will I do this summer? Will we be going anywhere? The Catskills, the Jersey shore?

Nope, it will be summer in the city for me.

For a fleeting moment, I think about telling Father Keenan the entire story—waking up from the fall, the brain insult, shadows, ghosts, Katherine, the nun in the boarding house once accused of witchcraft helping me get back into my body and teaching me to handle the shadows and the horsehead demons. I just want to get it off my shoulders.

Shit, you must be fucking stoned, Jack!

"Father? Dreams…" Father Keenan stops what he is doing and looks at me. He has started clearing the desk of his possessions; the space, after all, has been borrowed. Our time together is at an end. "Dreams…" I say again. "Never mind." I quickly add.

"No, continue. Dreams..." I have his complete attention.

"Do you think... Well, after my fall when I was out of it—I guess in a coma of sorts—I had a dream that my doctors..." I'm confused and not exactly sure what I want from him. "Forget it."

"Can you tell me what the dream was about?"

I am uncomfortable and squirm in the chair; I'm sorry I mentioned it.

"Do you read the Bible, Jack?"

I don't answer immediately, not sure where he is going with the question. "I mean I've read parts of the Bible," I say somewhat apologetically.

"The point is... the Bible is filled with prophets who had dreams." He leans in. "The verse that comes to mind is Daniel 1:17. 'As for these four young men, God gave them knowledge and skill in all literature and wisdom; and Daniel had understanding in all visions and dreams.' And of course, you have probably heard this one before. Matthew 2:13: 'After they had gone, an angel of the Lord appeared to Joseph in a dream and said: Arise, take the child and his mother and flee to Egypt, and stay there until I tell you, for Herod is going to look for the child to kill him.'"

We sit for a moment, and I feel as if something has been lifted from my shoulders. I see Father Keenan in a different light, a better light.

"Would you be comfortable telling me your dream?"

"It's not a big deal. Just a dream..." I have been so used to keeping secrets that even considering releasing one—no matter how helpful it might be—I find incredibly difficult. He sits for a moment waiting to see if I change my mind about telling him. Initially, I don't.

"I hope our meetings have been of some help to you, Jack," Father Keenan says, bringing our session to an end.

He hands me a business card. *I didn't know priests had business cards. Is this for his services as a priest? Or a psychologist? I guess it's kind of cool.*

"If you ever need spiritual guidance or just want to talk. High school can be very demanding," he says.

"Thank you." I put the card in my pocket.

I have the office door open and am ready to leave, but I decide to take a chance. To tell him.

"When I woke up from my fall, I thought I was married with a family. I could remember details about them. The doctors told me it was the injury to my brain that created it. My father said it was a dream."

"And you?"

"Yeah, I guess a dream."

Father Keenan looks at me before adding. "And Daniel could understand visions and dreams. Maybe a dream… maybe a vision of what is still to be."

It is in that moment that I know, for me, it is a new day and that I am thankful for having met Father Keenan. If not for any other reason than what he just said.

At the end of the school year, I can put everything aside to be normal for a moment. I enjoy all the graduation festivities—the dance, the ice cream social, our graduation breakfast, and classroom parties. It's fun. Most of my classmates and I have passed through school together since first grade. I love them. For her part, Sister Elizabeth does her best to neutralize our relationship and not show any hostility she may be harboring from all the crazy shit that happened. I am happy to just be normal for a while.

Three days after graduation, the Cairos leave for the Hudson Valley. All three of them attend my graduation, which really makes me emotional, because I know how awkward they must have felt. *I love Peter!* He hands me an envelope with a hundred-dollar bill in it; though, that's not the reason I love him. I love him because he never treated me like a stupid kid who didn't know anything. He wasn't afraid to say, "You're stronger than me in this area." *What would he have thought if I told him about Katherine and the kids?*

But these are all endings. Endings…

I watch through tears as the movers drive away from Stuyvesant Town, followed by the car with Peter and his parents. They wave and honk the car horn. *It is always harder for the people left behind. I need to concentrate on my new beginning in high school.*

The hot summer in the city heats up. Cohen has located Susan Michaels' cousin in Brooklyn. He asks me to take the train to Brooklyn with him, which I am happy about. I bring the only book I can find in the library with an image of Kasper's self-portrait, which is actually me. This photo is the only one published close to the time of the original sale. We meet at the subway station off 23rd Street and take the subway to 14th Street to get the L line to Brooklyn.

Along the way, Cohen wants to know how I came to know so much about Kasper Greenstreet and his art.

"We found the painting in Peter's storage," I reply. "I decided to find out everything about it and the artist that I could." *He will not get any backstory, just the facts.*

"Who discovered it?"

I could lie, which, quite frankly, I do a lot of the time. Although, I do not consider myself a liar. Only, if he already ran this by Peter, which is possible, it will prove me to be a liar. And he will not trust me. Besides, there is no reason to lie in this instance.

"Me. Peter had me hire someone to get into the storage because management never found the key to the lock."

"How did you start working for Peter?"

What does he want? I'm sick of people asking questions about Peter and me. "He needed someone to run errands for him and his parents. You know his dad was NYPD before his stroke," I say.

"Yes, I did know that…"

"Why did you leave the police force?" I ask, going on the offensive.

Detective Cohen looks at me. *Will he be honest?* "I had a problem with the bottle."

As we settle for our ride, I wonder if any of the shadows or demons will reveal themselves. *Are they gone now? Like Kasper?*

Susan Michaels' cousin, Mrs. Katie Walsh, is not what I expect. She is older, maybe in her late sixties. *It sounds stupid, because people age, but I expected a young person.* She lives in a small apartment not unlike the railroad flat my Dad and I share. It is nowhere near as nice as Peter's Gramercy Terrace apartment. *His old apartment, I should say.* The thought of that hurts. The woman makes us tea and offers a tin of cookies. Mrs. Walsh is very nice, and Cohen is very good with making her feel safe. He shows his private eye badge as well as his retired NYPD badge.

She places the tea down in front of us as she speaks.

"I thought Susan's estate was all settled."

"Oh, it is. We are here on another matter," Cohen says. "We're looking for records from the gallery she owned."

"Or photos of some of the artwork," I interject. "She represented the artists we are interested in. We just need to find out about a certain painting, the year it sold, that kind of stuff."

This woman looks at me as she puts the cookies down. "Who are you in all this?" Mrs. Walsh is not a fragile flower.

I show her my library book. "Working this summer to help pay my tuition for Xavier high school."

It's not a lie. I am still on Peter's payroll, which will pay something toward my tuition.

She keeps standing and leans against the refrigerator. "There was another man who showed up unannounced a couple of days ago, looking for similar information," she says.

"How so?" Detective Cohen asks.

"He wanted information on the gallery and Kasper Greenstreet. He asked if I have records of the people Susan sold Kasper Greenstreet's work to."

Cohen raises his eyebrows. "Did he leave you his name? A card?"

"Didn't give him a chance. He didn't call like you did; he just showed up. Something was not right with that guy."

"Can you tell us what he looked like?" I ask.

"Well, I didn't take the chain off my door. So, my view was limited. Wore a sport coat. He was nice looking, in a shady kind of way; I'll give him that."

The description she gives fits Mr. Philips.

"Do you have any paperwork from the gallery?" I ask.

"Maybe." She continues to assess us with her eyes, her own inner senses. "There are boxes down in the basement. I haven't gone through them personally."

"May we have a look?"

She leads us to the back of the hallway. A little neighbor boy, about six, comes out of his apartment down the hall and runs toward her. He is awkward, a little odd. She unlocks the basement door and flips on a light. All four of us make our way down the ancient staircase. The boy says nothing but makes a humming sound. Not surprisingly, the basement is far from neat. Boxes are piled in the corner, tarps and jars up against the far wall.

"Is that all of them?" Cohen asks hopefully.

"As far as I know. That's what was delivered from the lawyer after my cousin's estate was settled. I'll be upstairs getting my friend here some milk and cookies if you need me."

We divide the boxes. "What exactly are we looking for, Jack? I've never seen the painting."

Yeah, that's a problem. "If you come across any photos of art, give them to me. We want invoices with Kasper Greenstreet's name on them."

"Yeah, I get that," he says.

We spend hours in the basement, going through every box. We find tax records, Susan's mother's medical bills, and a lot of other items, but no photos of art or invoices for the sales of any art. Cohen finally sits on the basement steps, stretching his back. His age is catching up with him.

"We're striking out. What's left?" he asks, as I start attacking the last of the boxes.

"I think just these two."

The first box is not organized but appears to be filled with Polaroid pictures of paintings that hung at the Michaels' gallery. My heart beats faster. Some are random artists, but then I come across Polaroids of the *Duality* portrait and the *Pandora's Box* exhibit. There is the Polaroid of the Desiree Diamond painting—the one of her coming out of the TV like Botticelli's *Birth of Venus*. The next Polaroid is of a famous architect. Kasper painted him using parts from all the architect's famous buildings. I feel like I've hit pay dirt and I get lost in the Polaroid pictures that show these priceless paintings. Kasper painted two portraits—one was of their souls and was not flattering. As I continue to look, I begin to find bills of sale for the paintings themselves. The prices are ridiculous. *Makes me wonder how Kasper Greenstreet could have died broke.*

The last box contains more of Susan's mom's papers and one Manila envelope. I tear it open. Inside is the Holy Grail: the five Polaroid pictures of Kasper's self-portrait as a child and the bill of sale to the Countess Karlotta. For $255,000! There is also another legal document bequeathing the *Duality* self-portrait back to Kasper Greenstreet. It's stated value? $1.

"Oil!" I yell, jolting Cohen from a daydream and his aching back.

I bring everything over to him so he doesn't have to get up. "Peter should be here to interpret all this," he says.

"It's pretty clear," I say. "We can bring it to him."

"That's if the woman lets us leave with anything," he says, unaware of how important the find is.

"Shit, I didn't think of that."

"Don't even think about putting that under your shirt."

"Let's just ask her—beg her," I say, undeterred.

After we return to her apartment, I make an offer. "I can leave the book with you; this way you know we'll return," I say, like that is a proper deal.

Mrs. Walsh picks up the book. "It's a library book."

"Oh, damn." I'm coming off like a dumb shit but I'm just so excited.

"I like the triangle around your neck," she says.

Shit. I grab the pendant, not wanting to give it up. It's from Mr. David and carries so much meaning. But this is too important. We need these pictures and records.

As I start to remove it, she interrupts my action. "What does it mean? The triangle?"

"'The infinite power and protection of the Trinity,' according to the friend who gave it to me."

She stops me. "You keep it. You're young; you may need it."

We all get quiet. She picks up a pad by the telephone and writes down the inventory of the things we want. After a beat, she adds that we have two weeks to return the items or pay her $1,000. Both of us sign her handwritten promissory note, *which means... what? I definitely don't have $1,000, and I'm not sure the detective does, either.*

Behind the woman, the peculiar little boy sits there and stares, not saying a word. *Very odd little kid.*

Cohen grows tired on the train ride home. I'm amped and can't wait to call Peter. We have succeeded in our mission.

"Jack, I want to see the real painting," Cohen says through closed eyes.

"Thought you were napping?"

"Nope. Just resting." After a couple of beats, he adds, "It's probably time to give Mr. Philips a call. Find out exactly what he is up to. Obviously, he wants the same thing we do."

"Don't you think we should run this by Peter?"

"Can't do my job if I have to stop and ask permission every time. I need to make a move."

His point is well-taken, but I know I'll be calling Peter.

As soon as I get home, I telephone Peter and get a busy signal. The other day my dad blasted me for talking to the Cairos so much on the phone. "It's long distance, Jack. It's not cheap." When Peter sends me a check, I offer to pay Dad for the calls; he doesn't accept.

I keep calling until I finally speak to him. Peter has already spoken to our detective. *Guess he did need permission.*

"He's holding the Polaroids and the paperwork," I volunteer.

"Yes, he said he's going to make copies of the bill of sale. He said the other paper is a gift receipt or something to that effect."

"Essentially it gave ownership of the painting back to Kasper," I say.

"Yes, I want to look at it."

"Peter, our detective wants to see the real painting."

"Did he say why?"

"Not really. He also wants to meet with Mr. Philips."

"Yes, he told me."

Silence. "Can you come back to the city?" I ask. A long pause follows. "When we meet Mr. Philips?" I don't want to spook Peter because I do want to meet with Mr. Philips. I also know Mr. Philips is the one who tore up the apartment. "I'm not sure meeting with him is a good idea, but I think we must. "I add. "He apparently went out to Brooklyn to see about the painting. And then, of course, there is the break-in at your old apartment."

"Yes, Jack you going back for the painting was brilliant." Peter pauses for a moment. "Jack, when you show Cohen the painting, get the paperwork and the Polaroids from him. You already have a key to my personal P.O. Box; put them in there for now."

Cohen is waiting for me out front at the Chelsea area storage building on W. 23rd Street, where we are keeping the painting. *Should I be suspicious?* He has all the documentation and wants to meet with Mr. Philips, who's hot to buy the painting. Only Peter knows I'm meeting Cohen. *I could end up in the crate, while Cohen ends up with a painting worth a ton of money.* I touch the screwdriver in my pocket for a sense of security despite how false that security might be.

Cohen lets me open the crate while he watches. Together, we carefully take out the painting and unwrap it. Cohen takes a moment to view it, then steps back.

"It's disturbing," he says.

I guess it is, but at the same time, the color is so vibrant, otherworldly. You can't look away.

Cohen hands me the Polaroid pictures. I'm not an art expert but I know, even before I compare the photos, that they will match. The painting itself, though, has undergone a metamorphosis. It has changed drastically from the painting Uncle Willy and I removed from the basement storage that night. The first time I saw the painting, all you could see was a glimpse of the child. A hand, a lock of hair, the marbles. Shadows were engulfing him, smothering him, which I believe is what they did to Kasper during his life.

When I confronted Kasper in the apartment with the painting, the shadows slithered from the canvas like snakes out of a tree. They poured onto the floor, slid up the walls, and eventually shot straight from the painting onto the walls and ceiling. They revealed all of Kasper's fears, his shame, and his humiliation. It gave me the power to set his spirit free. In the end, when Kasper was gone, it became a beautiful painting of him as a child. Hopeful, in fact. In a supernatural way.

After I met Mr. Philips for the first time on the day of the sale at Peter's old apartment, the painting changed again. The outlines of the shadows began to reform. As I look at it now, it has reverted to the original painting, confirmed by the Polaroid pictures in my hands. Physically, the child looks like I did at that age. The psyche, however, is Kasper's. The three shadows sit just as he painted them. This is the reason Philips wants it. The painting is haunted, magical.

A sadness comes over me that I cannot quite define. *What was his intent? Was Kasper driven solely by inspiration or was his hope to exorcise the shadows, demons, and fears from his life by exposing them in his art? Did they take on a life of their own once he painted them? No longer servants of the artist? Did they become masters of his spirit and mind?*

I'm not afraid as I look at the Polaroid pictures. I've experienced this painting at its worst—and its best.

However, Cohen appears to be deeply troubled as he examines the painting carefully. "This sold for $255,000? That's crazy money," he utters, moving back and forth in the storage area, sweat forming on his brow. I pick up that Cohen is conflicted but I'm not sure exactly why. *The image in the painting? The money? His own intentions?*

As we leave, I continue holding the Manila envelope with the photos, original invoice, and documentation returning the ownership of the painting back to Kasper Greenstreet. The countess no longer wants anything to do with it. This is the paper Peter wants; it establishes the chain of ownership.

"Jack."

Detective Cohen motions for me to give him the envelope. I step away from him, prepared to run if need be.

"Peter wants me to place this in his P.O. Box," I say.

"You have the key?" he asks skeptically.

I nod.

"He never mentioned that to me."

"Well, you can call him; those are his instructions."

"Until I hear it from him, Jack, give me back the envelope," Cohen demands.

Everything in me switches to high alert. The blood moves in my veins. I step farther away.

He grows irritated. "Jack." I sense the thought of chasing me enters his head. He knows, however, that running after a fit 14-year-old boy is a losing proposition.

"Call him; call Peter." I continue to back away from him. When he stares me down, I turn and run. *Something is not right.*

Neither of us is aware that we are being watched. Someone has followed us, someone who wants the painting for more than its monetary value.

The P.O. Box that Peter rents is not far from my apartment. I walk there to place the envelope and its contents inside. I've been here before. Peter uses it for items he didn't want sent to the apartment or, now, to the Hudson Valley address. I never ask why.

Alone with Peter's P.O. Box, I am tempted to look at the other items inside. Some I can't help but see without officially prying—his wedding ring and an enclosed envelope with nothing written on it. I feel its contents; it could be money. Carefully, I place the Polaroids in the box. I move things around so they don't bend. Then I notice an open Manila envelope. It's not right, but I look anyway; it is the draft of a handwritten will. Everything is left to his parents—his life insurance policy, investments, and other assets. *As it should be.*

However, he has recently added the Kasper Greenstreet original painting to the will and left it to me.

Summer moves along quickly. Brick and I have rekindled our friendship. My dad is not happy and is very verbal about it. "It's not that I blame him for the fall…" *But of course, he does!* I understand Dad's feelings. He had to place all that fear and anger somewhere while sitting next to my hospital bed, watching me fight for my life. "But when you two are together..." he continues, "that's usually when the trouble starts."

Brick and I are staying out of trouble, but we are smoking a lot of pot. All we do is laugh. There are times when I wish I could tell Brick what the fall created in me—being able to see and hear things that very few people can see or hear, like shadows, spirits, people's fears, thoughts, smells.

My most pressing fear is going to Xavier and dealing with a curriculum that might be over my head in an environment of high-level competition. It is definitely bringing up anxiety in me. Smoking pot seems to comfort me and calm my nerves; only, it also dulls my abilities and intuition. I look over at Brick. *What are his fears?*

Peter wants me to mail the original bill of sale and gifting of the painting to him for his court filing. He has filed under the Abandoned Property Law, referring to property to which the owner has relinquished all rights. "When property is abandoned, the owner gives up the reasonable expectation of privacy concerning it. The person finding the abandoned property is entitled to keep it." That is Peter's legal approach.

"Make copies before you mail them to me. Wait, why don't you come up for a couple of days? Mom and Pop really miss you. You can get out of the city..."

I love the idea. My dad makes several telephone calls with Peter and Julia before the arrangements are finalized. Peter insists on paying for everything.

Grand Central Station is one of the crowns of New York architecture in a city with plenty of architectural marvels to choose from. It was built in the Beaux-Art style in 1913 and has forty-four platforms and sixty-seven tracks. One can happily get lost inside, spending the day admiring all it has to offer. The Vanderbilt food court can accommodate breakfast, lunch, dinner, and cocktails while passengers wait, or just hang out.

The main concourse features an amazing barrel-vaulted ceiling containing a mural of constellations. Apparently, there are astronomical inaccuracies;

some stars and constellations appear correctly on the ceiling while others are reversed. Ten globe-shaped chandeliers hang from the constellation-filled ceiling, weighing eight hundred pounds each and holding approximately one hundred and ten light bulbs. Once during a school trip, they were lowered for cleaning. The four-faced brass clock has made its appearance in many movies and television shows. *All amazing!*

While carrying my small suitcase with the Polaroids and documents tucked between my underwear and socks, I feel the presence of someone or something following me. I step into one of the stores and buy a chocolate bar and pretzels for my ride up the Hudson. I look around to see if and what I'm picking up. I can't seem to shake a sense of danger, but no one reveals themselves. *Nothing.* I find my way to Platform 23 and board my train for what becomes a beautiful ride along the Hudson. *I can't wait to see everyone.*

When I arrive at the train station, Peter is waiting for me. We drive to their new house—a small cottage outside of a small town. Julia greets me like I am her grandchild. Long gone is the question mark that used to appear over Mr. Cairo when he sees me. Now, I am greeted with an old fashion Jack in the Box windup toy over his head. Instead of a clown, though, a bear comes out of the box. *Glad it's not a clown; only, I do miss the question mark.*

Peter is so relaxed I barely recognize him. He is a million miles away from the last days of New York—from that Peter. Julia makes dinner while Peter and I ride around on bikes. It is a beautiful, old town with a main street all of two blocks long. I remember Brick telling me once that, when he moved out of New York City, he was bored shitless. But this is nice. Peter and I park the bikes and stroll along Main Street. We grab ice cream, promising neither of us will tell Julia. In the morning, Peter and Julia make breakfast and brew coffee and tea.

After breakfast, Peter wants to see the documents. I unwisely pour everything out of the envelope onto the table—a rather foolish mistake. Julia picks up the Polaroids, looks through them, and hands them to Peter.

He immediately drops the pictures like they have burned his hands. "I don't want that!"

It's hard to get the toothpaste back in the tube once it's been squeezed. What has been seen cannot be unseen. Peter goes into a tailspin. "Why did you give me that?" Peter yells at Julia. "Why are you touching this stuff?" *Is a touch of hysteria returning to his psyche?*

He turns to me. "Why did you bring those pictures here?"

I apologize. It is all I can do. On the one hand, Julia thinks he's being ridiculous and says so; only, she doesn't understand what those shadows did to him, the mess they made of him.

Quickly, I pack the Polaroids into the envelope and hide them in my suitcase. I leave the documents I know he wants and needs on the dining room table. However, Peter has gone sideways. Our once promising weekend is over. He stays locked up in his room all day Saturday. Julia spends the rest of Saturday emptying boxes from their move. They are living in a rural area, which encourages me toward the decision to push Mr. Cairo around the neighborhood in his wheelchair to stay out of both of their ways. There are no sidewalks, but the streets are asphalt.

We begin with a nice leisurely walk. We come along a wooded area with a creek on the opposite side of the road. Very peaceful. Up ahead, there is movement from the woods. *A wolf? Coyote?*

What looks like a large dog trots onto the street. A bunch of question marks appear over Mr. Cairo's head. *They do not represent me.* The animal begins to walk slowly toward us. *It is definitely a wolf.* I stop immediately once it begins to growl. I've heard wolves howl in movies but never like this. It's intimidating.

I hear Mr. Cairo's thoughts. *Back away slowly but don't turn around, Jack. Maintain eye contact.*

There is no image over his head. Just a clear thought. I follow his instructions. The wolf continues to growl and snarl but does not come after us. We back all the way up the street until the wolf fades from sight.

We have a light dinner and then play cards at the table in the backyard. We play Crazy Eights, Blackjack, and Rummy. Mr. Cairo goes to bed early and watches television. Julia and Peter are better, not as agitated, but not as they were when I first arrived.

It is a nice night after a day of tension. Peter is apologetic; the scars left over from Kasper Greenstreet run deep. I make no mention of the wolf encounter, even as several cats appear in the yard, meandering for mice, I guess. Neither Peter nor Julia make mention of them. I assume feral cats and wolves are part of the area's natural habitat.

"Rummy," Peter says, showing us his winning hand.

Julia asks if we want to play a board game. Monopoly? The Game of Life? Peter raises his eyebrows when he suddenly realizes the yard has ten to fifteen cats roaming around. "Mom? Where did all these cats come from?"

Now it's Julia's turn to be surprised. "Let's go in," she says.

"This is not normal?" I ask. I'm sorry I did. Peter looks at me with suspicion.

There are no more games. We all retire for the night. A lone cat sits outside my window, hissing most of the night. I am the last one to fall asleep and the last one to wake. The Cairos are all up having breakfast when I get up. They will be going to church. I ask them to drop me off at the train station; I'm ready to get back to the city.

Brick and I spend our days going to Rye Beach and Coney Island, having a blast. We have begun dating the Taper sisters. Brick is dating the older sister, Annette, while I am dating Ann. They match our ages, fifteen and seventeen. My birthday was July 3rd, but I always wished I had been born on the 4th. The line of the song "Yankee Doodle Dandy" runs through my head: "A real live nephew of my Uncle Sam/Born on the 4th of July."

Brick and I are always riding the subways. Nothing comes out to mess with me anymore. However, the voices are back, some very strong. When I say voices, I mean the thoughts of people or maybe even the voices of their deceased loved ones. *Are they trying to relay a message?* Sometimes, they're too loud, especially when Brick and I are having fun. The marijuana lowers the volume, which is good and bad, because I find myself reaching for a joint at all times of the day. But the good thing is it also helps me with my migraines.

One night, the girls, Brick, and I head out to Coney Island. On the beach, we smoke a joint rolled in hash oil before going on the boardwalk. Our first ride is the Wonderworld, where we have plenty of time for kissing. Next is Spook-a-Rama. Brick sits in his car with Annette. Ann and I share another car. It is a typical boardwalk spook ride, filled with flashing lights and mechanical bogeymen. Ann and I do a lot of kissing. When we kiss, it is always French kissing. She gave me a hickey once, which sent my father into waves of laughter.

"Who gave you the love bite, Jack? When do I get to meet her?"

At some point in the ride, the music and sounds in the haunted house slow down so much it becomes distorted. The ride itself seems to be moving in slow motion. *The weed?* I stop with the kissing and let go of her.

A figure seems loose in the darkness. It seems like an illusion, part of the ride, until he sticks his head into our car and calls out my name. The darkness and strobe light alter my facial recognition. It's a man, but I cannot make out his face. I scream, which makes Ann scream. The man is gone as fast as he came, but he leaves with words that sound like "I want it!"

The face I don't know. The voice I do. Mr. Philips.

From time to time, I find myself really missing Peter and Mr. David. They were both my mentors in very different ways. I would not have survived eighth grade without them. Sister Elizabeth comes to my mind more than I would like. I've even had a dream about her. She is walking down 2nd Avenue, her nun's habit blowing gently behind her. I'm running, trying to catch up to her, wanting—no, needing—to tell her something. Some force or wind is holding me back. Nothing comes out of my mouth when I yell to her. I don't know what it means or if it even means anything.

I'm hoping for a call from Peter or Cohen. I'm not sure what we are doing now with the painting or what they want to do. *Is Philips someone we need to speak with? Do we want to get information? And why is he after the same information on the painting? I'm intrigued by him but, at the same time, very leery.*

Peter calls me. We set up a meeting with Mr. Philips for the last week of summer.

Reluctantly, Peter makes the trek back to the city. His parents still keep the apartment in Stuyvesant Town, just in case living away from the city doesn't work out. Plus, there is rent control, and they've been in the apartment for thirty years. How do you give that up? The plan is for Detective Cohen and I to meet Peter at the apartment to go over a few items.

Arriving at the apartment before Cohen, I find Peter very tense, like he was when he saw the Polaroids of the painting during my weekend visit. He doesn't miss the city or any of this drama with Kasper Greenstreet.

"I'm not sure why we are meeting this guy. I have no plans to sell the painting," Peter says the minute I walk in.

I'm a little disappointed because this cloak-and-dagger shit is kind of exciting to me. "Peter, it's your call," I reply.

"Yes, I know, but this detective—Cohen—keeps pressuring me. I should have let all this play out in the legal system." That's where Peter is most comfortable, behind a desk, preparing briefs.

"What do you want to do?" I ask.

"What can I do? Everything is in motion!" He's snappy.

"Peter, we don't have to show up."

"Cohen wants me to meet him alone. He doesn't think you should be there."

"Because?"

"Because you are a kid."

"He didn't mind having me with him when we went out to Brooklyn to meet with Susan Michaels' cousin to look through the paperwork. Which, by the way, I found before bringing him to the storage and showing him the painting. He was okay with all of that."

"Cohen was pissed about you running off with the pictures and documents."

"Did you tell him you needed them?"

"Yes. He still felt you were disrespectful."

"Well, I'm the only one who has met Mr. Philips and knows what he looks like." I say, shrugging my shoulders. "I have to be there."

"You and I know that. Cohen's plan is to wait outside and follow Mr. Philips after we meet with him."

"Wait a minute—Cohen's not going to be in the meeting?" *Suspicious.*

"No. He keeps asking me why I don't want to sell? Get all that money? Of course, he doesn't know what we know about the painting."

"So, he will have no active involvement with this meeting," I say, digesting this new development. "And he wanted you to go alone?"

Peter nods. "Don't let the detective trouble you, Jack. You and I know what you can do; that's all that matters."

With that, he reaffirms that we really are the partners in this, not Cohen, who I do not trust. "Peter, I put the Polaroid pictures back in the P.O. Box. Do you want the keys?"

"No, I want you to hold on to them for me."

The three of us do not travel together to the West Side docks, where the meeting takes place. Peter and I are to meet Mr. Philips at some shithole diner. Cohen is going to be right outside if we need him. Mr. Philips chose the place, which does not equate with his demeanor or physical presence. Our detective will float around, waiting for his chance to follow Mr. Philips when we are done. He has not been able to locate an address on Mr. Philips or his business. Nothing. *This is his chance, but for what?*

Peter wants to take a cab; I suggest walking, hoping the walk will loosen him up. We're running late, so it's a taxi ride.

The diner is set back off the West Side Highway. It looks as out of place as Mr. Philips did that first day I met him in the apartment. As soon as we open the door to the diner, I am hit with a wave, a current, a vibration, a pulsating energy—one of the strangest energies I have ever experienced. It goes through my body, blood, and DNA and leaves me on high alert. Peter does not feel any of this because his own energy is all over the fucking place. *How can he pick up on anything else? I wish he would calm the fuck down and not be so overwhelmed. He is a liability.*

Peter looks around, befuddled. I'm afraid he might break, spill out right here on the floor.

Big red booths are affixed to the walls of the diner, with individual tables in the middle of the room. A long lunch counter sits empty. There are just a few people in the place.

Peter is not sure who we are looking for, so I take control. "This way," I say, heading toward Mr. Philips, who sits at a table.

Mr. Philips is the center of the vortex, the source of the vibration. The pulsating energy is coming from him. He stares straight ahead but not directly at us, trance-like, though aware we are walking toward him. He does not get up from the table to greet us. *There is something completely in-between about this guy. Clearly, he is earthbound, but Vampiresque? If that is even such a fucking thing. Necromancer? Witch? Fucked-up human being?* I can't help cursing inside; for some reason, it is relaxing to me. Keeps me focused. "Don't worry about him cursing, Mr. Kelly. That's not unusual after a head injury!" The doctors had said. Everything comes back to my fall, even my foul language.

"Jack, who also plays," are the first words out of his mouth.

"Mr. Philips."

We lock eyes. It could be viewed as a childish staring contest; only, it is much more than that.

With the risk of sounding like a complete douchebag, I have lived multiple lives since my fall. Battled demons, shadows, and a real live fucking ghost. Yes, I have learned a little about who I am and the people around me.

This man is a danger.

Peter distracts me. It is abundantly clear that the vibration pulsing from this dude has thrown Peter off his newfound peace. His orbit is spinning off course. Mr. Philips and I wait for Peter to speak, but he doesn't. I place my hand on Peter's arm to encourage him, to settle him down.

Mr. Philips sees an opening. He immediately takes advantage. "I was pleasantly surprised to hear from you," he says directly to Peter. "Since Jack here told me the painting was not for sale, I thought the kid was in charge."

Ouch! Peter is mute. Looking over at him, I want to tell him to snap out of it. "Peter," I say softly.

Finally, he finds his voice. "We are exploring our options," he says. "It seems you've been making inquiries with people who cannot actually help you. If you would like to make an offer, or an inquiry, I'm a lawyer. And as you are well aware, I am in possession of the painting, it..." He stumbles over the words. "...will be mine."

Mr. Philips' skin is translucent; the veins in his face, head, and hands are clearly visible. And twitching. I can almost see the blood flow from the outside of his body. *Maybe he is a vampire.* His demeanor changes; I sense a man who can easily commit violence, even murder. Peter is not reading any of this as he continues talking, rambling.

Finally, Peter says, "You seem to have great interest in the painting. May I ask why?"

Mr. Philips looks at Peter like he would like to tear his windpipe out. For a moment, I think he's going to, which makes me feel like a fucking kid. I'm hit with a wave of fear—*how badly am I outmatched?* I slowly handle the fork in front of me, inspecting its tines, because *if this motherfucker makes a move toward Peter, I am prepared to stick it in his eye.*

None of our thoughts escape Mr. Philips. He looks at me just as I've finished that thought. He thinks in moving images, somewhat like Mr. Cairo but on steroids. His gaze switches from Peter to me like he is prepared for hand-to-hand combat. However, it is very clear that this battle is taking place on a spiritual level, not an actual fistfight. Some kind of sorcery here. I become keenly aware that Mr. Philips is a psychic, a magician, an energy vampire. He can steal your thoughts, emotions, and power. He's not a shadow, but... *what?* Certainly an entity like none I've previously experienced or battled.

I must tap into all of it—the shadows, demons, what I learned from Kasper Greenstreet, and what the nun taught me. I must unravel his secret, the source of his power. Most importantly, while in his presence, I must house my thoughts in the injured part of my brain, where they tell me I created Katherine, my kids. My thoughts are untouchable there. I don't want him to see what I'm thinking or feeling at the diner table. I must place them in that untouchable place.

My fear is not for my safety. My fear is that he will destroy someone I love before I've figured out how to fight him. Mr. Philips, like Kasper Greenstreet, knows that Peter is no match. *But me? Kasper thought I was a demon. What does Mr. Philips think? He must know I am the one he must contend with.* I am torn between wanting to protect Peter and getting down and dirty with Mr. Philips. I must be smart and patient. It took me too much time to figure out Kasper. It cost me Mr. David's friendship and resulted in Peter moving away, alienating myself from half my classmates and Sister Elizabeth and led to fighting with my father. I became somewhat of a pariah at Epiphany, the school I love so much. *This time, I must be better prepared. Ready for battle with ghosts, demons, witches, shadowy creatures. And this motherfucker!*

Mr. Philips is sucking the energy from Peter, who has begun to hunch, as if disappearing from his own power. "You may ask me anything you want," Philips finally says. "But I have a question for you. What do you think of the painting, Peter?"

He knows full well Peter has not viewed the painting. *I know that he knows but I'm not sure how exactly.*

Peter's reaction validates his hunch. He freezes. "I... um..."

Mr. Philips stares, his eyes mirroring a weak period in Peter's life: being hauled off to Bellevue. He's not reading Peter's mind, but rather, his biography. Peter doesn't see the mirroring but feels it.

Not good. "Did you see the painting for the first time in the apartment?" I interrupt, trying to deflect whatever spell he is putting on Peter. "Your reaction was intense." Mr. Philips continues staring at Peter. "Did you know Kasper Greenstreet personally?" I ask, trying to disturb the connection. *It's not working.* I touch Peter firmly to arouse him from this spell.

Now Philips looks at me, menace in his eyes and obliteration on his mind. I'm afraid but ready.

Suddenly, napkins, menus, and newspapers begin to blow wildly around the diner. Several chairs blow over from the maelstrom Philips is creating. This does not emerge from confusion or frustration, which is what I've seen over Mr. Cairo's head, nor is it the pure anger of Kasper Greenstreet. This is a combination of rage and power. A dose of *look at what I can do!* Philips' eyes change to the lightest color blue I have ever seen. Mirrors. Only, the image reflecting back at me is that of a powerful warrior. Not some fifteen-year-old boy.

He quickly turns the mirror off. *Is it so I don't see how powerful I am? Or is he toying with me, giving me a false sense of self?*

The black magician's tricks have Peter backing away in his seat. His image in Mr. Philips eyes is that of a mouse, and Peter feels it! The cats scampering around the property on the Hudson reflect in Philips' eyes.

"Afraid of a little wind, Peter? What are you, a mouse?" Mr. Philips asks.

What is this guy? How do I bring this fucker down?

The witchcraft does not faze other diners. Mr. Philips chose this place for a reason. It hits me that we are in a den of witches, warlocks, and sorcerers and not the good kind.

Philips looks at me with a sly, seductive smile filled with evil intent. Slowly I pull the triangle out from under my shirt saying the words loud enough for him to hear. "The infinite power, protection of the Trinity." *I want Mr. Philips to see and feel the triangle, but I'm not sure why.*

All the chaos and wind stop. He holds his sly smile with great difficulty while looking from me to Peter and back to me.

A long silence follows before he says, "I've seen that thing around your neck before." He is visibly irritated.

"You couldn't have; it's one of a kind," I say dismissively, letting him see that I am lying. Intentionally.

The stare of a hungry lion ready to eat replaces his sly grin. "No, no I've seen it before, somewhere in Turkey. Istanbul?"

Exactly where Mr. David found it. Time to change the subject. "Are you hungry Mr. Philips? Would you recommend the pie at this place?" I ask, knowing full well Peter and I will eat nothing; I say it to inform Philips I can read thoughts as well, pick up on his lion's appetite.

The door to the diner opens and slams several times, startling Peter. He seems to be shrinking in his seat. He's finished. I try and keep myself unfazed by Mr. Philips' parlor tricks.

"Are you planning to make us an offer?" I ask, completely in charge of this side of the table.

It would be great fun to tell him that Kasper threw way more than this little charade at me. But more wind and fireworks follow. Doors open and slam, and chairs are blown around. A fork comes flying toward Peter, which I catch and weaponize.

Mr. Philips is prepared for violence.

Now I understand why Kasper thought I was a demon because typical humans do not pick up on another's energy, do not see their damaged souls. Once you do, it alters the power structure. Kasper didn't understand initially that I was from the light; he was actually looking for the light. Mr. Philips' plan is to extinguish the light!

He looks at me, flashing the image of my girlfriend and I in the haunted house at Coney Island. Then he stands, directing his rant at Peter. "The way I make my inquiries about the possible purchase of art is my affair. Don't ever question me!"

"Okay," Peter says, meekly as a frightened lamb ready for slaughter. He is completely overwhelmed. I'm afraid, too, but I fight not to show it, to reveal anything Philips can use against me.

"You want to sell the painting," Mr. Philips says, like he is ordering it. Or issuing a warning. "Talk. Only, stop being a pussy and leave the boy at home next time."

I don't know exactly what you want, Mr. Philips, with that painting, but I can guess. To unleash those shadows to give you even more black magic.

"I want that painting. And you will want to give it to me eventually!"

Fuck you! Can you read that, Mr. Philips? We will never sell you that painting.

I show him an image of me burning the painting, which alarms him. He looks at me for what I've become to him: enemy number one.

Finally, Mr. Philips leaves through the kitchen. We stay seated till he's gone. An echo moves through the diner. The rest of the patrons—witches, warlocks, magicians—are now keenly aware of the battle looming between us. There is excitement in their vibration.

"What the fuck was that?" Peter says.

Putting my finger to my lips, I motion for him to be quiet. We get up and leave.

On the way back to Stuyvesant Town, we debrief. Peter is a basket case and has decided to take the train back up the Hudson to the safety of his new home. He wants to get out of the city as soon as he can. He wants nothing to do with this voodoo. "Should we just burn that painting, Jack?" he asks.

"We should have done it before you filed all the paperwork," I say. "What if we burn it and it unleashes whatever evil is in the painting?"

Peter is teetering. I hope he is not Bellevue bound. "Yes, yes—you're right. That guy was so eerie. He's not dead, right?" Peter asks. "Because... wow! What's happening?"

"No." I speak confidently, but it's a lie. It's obvious Mr. Philips is into voodoo, black magic, and maybe even has a pact with the devil to keep himself earthbound. *But what is he, exactly? I'm not sure.* He was completely aware of the hoard of cats at Peter's house. He also knew Peter had never seen the painting.

I fix my eyes on Peter. "We need to stay away from him. Make sure he never gets that painting; he only has evil intentions. Playing with some kind of voodoo."

We walk quietly; Peter is shivering, but it is summertime and hot. "Did you see Cohen when we came out of the diner?" he asks.

"No. I thought he was going to follow Mr. Philips."

"Well, I'm going to pay him for his service. Tell him his work with us is done. I need to be finished with all of this, Jack, or it will destroy me."

Back at the apartment, an unsteady Peter pulls his overnight bag together in a hurry.

"I'd like to move the painting to a different storage," I say.

Peter looks at me. "Why?"

"Just a really strong feeling like I had the time I removed it from your old apartment." I don't trust Mr. Philips—or Detective Cohen. "Do you want me to take the train back home with you?"

"No, Jack, I'll be fine. Just have to get out of the city. Triggers too many things for me."

I insist on walking Peter to Grand Central Station to make sure he gets on the train safely. He hugs me tightly before boarding the train. "Jack, it is I who should be protecting you."

I decide to wait until he is safely on the train, looking around to make sure neither Mr. Philips nor Cohen followed us. As Peter gets on the train, I survey the tunnel for horsehead demons and shadows. Nothing. They're from a previous dream; one that has dissipated.

Peter takes a seat and waves as the train slowly pulls out. Through the train car window, I see Mr. Philips on the other side of the platform, standing and watching. Then he's gone. I catch a glimpse of a passenger on the last car—*could it be Mr. Philips?* Across from the track on the platform, another man glides toward the stairs. *Him again?*

My mind is playing tricks on me.

PETER CAIRO

Peter got onto the train feeling shame and fear; all his serenity shattered by this trip to the city. *I'm weak. I can't handle or understand any of these things. Ghosts? Black magic? What I experienced at the Gramercy Terrace sent me to the psych ward.* Peter sees Jack from the window of his train, standing there protectively, like some warrior from a long-lost tribe of angels. This confuses Peter more. Had Peter not lived it clearly, he would think it insane. His stint in Bellevue confirmed the insanity of it all. However, the fact that there are other witnesses— Jack for one—makes his story true. As for Jack's mystic friends? Peter has not met them.

Jack seems to bear no trauma from the incident when Peter chased him around the apartment with a butcher knife. He holds no animosity, no grudge. Incident—the word itself is bullshit, and Peter knows it. *It was a psychotic break. How could he do that to Jack?* Peter loves him like a brother, a son even…

What Peter remembers from that day is he was sitting on the couch when Jack let himself into the apartment. The two spoke, but the words are lost to Peter now. There were things on the walls—shadows, if his memory is correct. They had been there for days. Peter's endless nights of insomnia were followed by days filled with paranoia and delusions. It became a split screen in a movie theater, some madman chasing this kid around the apartment. Paralyzed, Peter had sat on the couch watching, no participation, connection, or way to stop it. He was of no help to this kid. It was as if Peter was… possessed. *Only, now it is as real as this train pulling out of Grand Central Station.*

There were shadows jumping on and off walls, whispering. That guest room was possessed, haunted. Jack seemed to have an answer to their mayhem. He told Peter not to go back into that bedroom. In fact, it was very much like today, with Jack bringing him to the train station. That night he walked Peter to 2nd Avenue, hailed a cab, put him in it, and sent him to his parents' apartment; only, Peter didn't go.

Peter returned to the apartment. The shadows lured him to listen outside the door, speaking lies about Jack, how little they thought of Peter. Trying to get away from the voices, Peter went to bed looking for comfort. It did not come. After just a few hours of sleep, he woke up to find an art show going on in his living room. Kasper Greenstreet was there. *It felt real; it still feels real.* Like Peter had walked in to some other dimension, some alternate reality. Not déjà vu, but a parallel universe. Sliding into crazy. As if that party was happening simultaneously with the present. Stepping into the living room from the master bedroom, it was more surreal than unreal. Kasper's paintings of well-known people, rich people in two different lights—Desiree Diamond among them—lined the walls.

Then Peter came upon a painting of himself. He did not like what it revealed about him. All the time, these people kept saying, "He's genius; he'll paint who you really are." Peter found himself walking through the party naked, through the lobby of the building, the garden. It was as if he had split in two. One was the watcher, one the doer, and Peter was lost somewhere in-between.

Coming back to the city was clearly a mistake. Peter and his parents had found a level of peace in their small little town along the Hudson. Except for the weekend Jack visited, but that was not his fault. Peter knows he is not fully himself yet, but he is beginning to feel settled living with his parents, which at his age seems weird. He knows he must block this from his mind—convince himself it is all temporary and that, eventually, he will move out and find someone to love. Peter and Julia have planted a small herb garden. He's even done a little law work for the local attorney. Together they have been working with Peter's father, making him exercise.

After Jack left that weekend, Julia found coloring books in a box she was emptying. Jack had been using them to work with Peter's dad on improving his writing and dexterity. It was an amazing level of progress. In the beginning, Mr. Cairo could only scribble. Pure scribble in the beginning. Then he made it between the lines, but childish. Finally, he colored some of the most beautiful pictures, with bold colors. Just lovely. Julia and Peter were stunned. She blurted out that Jack had a gift. "He's an old soul in a boy's body." *She's right, but she still has no idea what he truly understands and can do.* Even now as close as they've become, Peter would not dare tell her any of the things that went on in the apartment at Gramercy Terrace. All this occult black magic talk would spook her for sure. Just as it spooks Peter.

When will it end? This painting will legally be his in just a short period of time. He's already insured it. It has to be worth a lot of money, but Jack and Peter believe it should never see the light of day. *What selling it could pay for... a house, college for Jack, even retirement.* However, Peter and Jack both agreed that would be the wrong thing to do.

Who is this Philips that showed up to buy it out of the blue, holding a past connection to Kasper Greenstreet? All that crazy shit in the diner? Witchcraft? Peter knows he needs to distance himself from all this and concentrate fully on getting well.

He closes his eyes and lets the train rock him to sleep.

Peter is back in the Gramercy Terrace apartment on the night of Kasper Greenstreet's art show. There is a man with his back to him, getting ready to pull a beautiful red curtain off one of the paintings on the wall.

"Don't you want to see it?" he asks loudly.

No, I don't think I want to see it. Peter steps back from him, from the painting.

"Yes, you do! You want to see it!" His voice is familiar.

Peter shakes his head slowly then violently, but words will not come. Mr. Philips pulls the curtain away from the painting. "Ta da!" The images in the painting are moving, with Peter in straitjacket, fighting to get free.

Mr. Philips throws back his head and laughs. "Don't you love it? Don't you just love it? It's you!" Mr. Philips turns to face him with a most wicked smile.

Peter's head shakes vehemently, like it's going to explode from his body. The movement transcends the dream, spreads into Peter sitting on the train, waking him from the nightmare. Across is a man who, for a moment, Peter thinks is Philips. He pants, his heart racing with the thought. The man is startled and stares suspiciously at him over his newspaper.

He needs to wash his hands from this entire thing, but how can he? He regrets not having burned the fucking painting the minute Jack described it to him. Now, they must keep it locked away as if it is some living organism with a power all its own. Jack has been true to his word, releasing Kasper Greenstreet's hold on the apartment. In the diner, Jack seemed keenly aware but not overwhelmed by Philips or any of his magic. Or witchcraft. Or whatever the fuck it was. Peter can't help but think this man will undo Jack and that there is nothing he can do about it.

The train rolls into the station. Peter sees his mother sitting on the hood of the car. His dad is patiently waiting in the passenger seat for him. Home.

JACK KELLY

Uncle Willy meets me at the storage unit. We move the painting to a unit closer to Dad's and my apartment. Uncle Willy and I are the only ones who know its new location. I don't even tell Peter because he doesn't want to know. I put the receipt in Peter's P.O. Box just to leave a trail.

It's time for school. My freshman year of high school starts off the way my eighth-grade year ended—messy. Immediately, I feel like an outsider; although, I put myself in the position to feel that way. After two weeks of picking up thoughts and emotions from students and faculty, I've begun smoking pot on the way to school just to quiet the noise. September fades into October without notice. I'm already behind with several assignments. *This passive aggressive bullshit is hurting me, but I don't feel like putting in the work to quiet the voices on my own. Using the tools Mr. David taught me could save some grief in the long run, but smoking a joint is easier, faster. Besides that, I like the buzz.*

Brother Thomas is droning on in my religion class. I'm not sure exactly how long I've mentally stepped away from his lecture. I'm still sitting in class, trying to figure out a way to disappear physically. If I could, I would. Complaining of headaches does not work with the brothers the way it did with Sister Thaddeus and Sister Elizabeth at Epiphany. Even when my headaches get bad, they tell me I need to endure. "Take an Excedrin."

Peter called last night wondering if I'd heard from Detective Cohen. Peter sent him a letter with a check, thanking him for his service and notifying him that his work for us was done. That was several weeks ago.

"The check has not been cashed," Peter says, "and Cohen hasn't returned any of my phone calls. Has he contacted you, Jack?"

"No, he hasn't called me since we went to Brooklyn… wait, no, since we made plans for him to see the painting." A long pause follows. "He never contacted you after following Mr. Philips?" I ask.

"No," Peter says, clearly wanting to be finished with all of this. "Last time we spoke was the day we went to the diner."

A hard knock on the classroom door brings me back. A senior boy I've seen around campus walks in with a note and hands it to Brother Thomas. Brother barely glances at the note before pointing to me. "Kelly, the dean would like to see you." Immediately, I sober up. *"Would like to see you"—does that mean it's optional?*

On the way down the stairs, I imagine that someone has told on me for smoking a joint on the way to school or seen me somewhere taking a hit. I start thinking up a bullshit story. *I'll say it's medicinal, for my headaches. Clearly, it's illegal, so I doubt that's going to fly.* Outside the dean's office, I take a deep breath and get ready to go into the full "poor me" role. I almost died, blah, blah, blah, but even I'm bored with that routine. *Are you a warrior, Jack, or a frightened child? Can I be both?*

When I slowly open the door to his office, I immediately pick up a completely different level of energy in the room. Two men are seated inside, waiting for me. Cops. My mind begins taking mental inventory of the inside of my locker, scanning it in my head… *do I have any pot? Paraphernalia these guys could find?*

"Jack Kelly."

"Yes, sir." *I've been so stupid and careless with this shit like I want to get caught.*

"Come in, Mr. Kelly," the dean says, pointing to a chair. *Don't speak, Jack; let them talk first.* "These men are detectives," the dean says.

I shake their hands like a proper little gentleman. Detective Gruff shows me a picture of Detective Cohen. "Do you know this man?" he asks.

I look at the two detectives. "Yes. Did something happen?"

"When was the last time you saw him?"

"Is he dead?" I ask, already knowing the truth.

The dean does not like the word "dead" and jumps in with a question of his own. "Shouldn't you be doing this with his father present?"

Detective Gruff continues as if he's deaf to our questions. "Can you tell us the last time you saw him?" he asks again.

"Hmm. It's been a while."

"Can you be more specific?"

I have a bad feeling. "How did he die?" I ask. *I am clearly picking something up.*

"Detective, doesn't he need his father here?" the dean asks again, more firmly.

"Can you tell me how he died?" I repeat.

Finally, the other detective chimes in. "He was found floating in the East River."

Oh shit! "You know he's an ex-cop," I say, like I'm adding value to the investigation.

"Yes, we are aware of that. Now, I would like to know the last time you saw Mr. Cohen."

The dean stops staring at the detectives and puts his attention on me. *This is not the way I want to get on the dean's radar. Have they contacted Peter?*

"Detectives. I really must insist that you do this kind of questioning in the presence of his father!" The dean now says in a commanding way.

No, no. Question me right here, right now! My father doesn't know any of this shit! This is not good. It is one more thing to disappoint my father, another reason for him to be pissed at me.

But the dean has his way.

Soon, my father and I are sitting in the police station, waiting for the detectives to settle in. They have a picture of Mr. Cohen on the desk, the one they showed me at school. They also have several pictures of him after he was pulled out of the East River. I know it's ridiculous, inappropriate even, but I can't help but think of a line from *The Godfather*: "It's a Sicilian message. It means Luca Brasi sleeps with the fishes."

In this case, I believe the message is from Mr. Philips. Sorcerer. Black magician. It's all related; I just know it is. This will set Peter back—maybe lead to another stint in the psych ward.

"What was your relationship with the deceased?" the detective asks, as if we hadn't skipped a beat from the questioning at school.

My father spots the photos of the dead man. "Can you turn those over? He doesn't need to see that."

"Of course. Sorry," says the detective who told me Cohen was dead. Detective Gruff waits for me to answer.

I have him ask the question again. "In what capacity did you know him?"

"He worked for us," I reply.

Peter told me something a long time ago from a lawyer's point of view, something I always try to keep in mind, especially when someone is questioning me. "If you are asked for information, don't elaborate. If someone asks if you know the time, say 'yes.' The question is not, 'can you tell me what time it is?' The question is, 'do you know the time?' 'Yes.' Don't give the time; that's a different question."

The detective looks at my father, who looks at me. "Worked for you, Mr. Kelly?" the detective asks my father.

"No—for Peter and me," I interrupt.

This is going to become a shit show. Peter didn't pick up when I called him after school. I tried him right before Dad and I had to leave for the police station.

"Peter?" The other detective jumps in. "Peter Cairo?"

"Yes." *I'm not sure how much to tell them. Should I play the dopey teenager?*

"Were you paying him, or was Peter Cairo paying him?"

"Peter."

"So, when you say, 'he was working for us,' you mean he was working for Peter Cairo?"

"Okay."

"Okay what?" Gruff is already running out of patience with me.

My father stares at me like I've just landed from another planet.

"Isn't this all semantics?" I ask, as respectfully as possible. "I mean, isn't the important thing here to find out who killed Mr. Cohen?"

All three men—my father and the two detectives—give me that look, which I've seen before from a wide variety of adults. The look that practically screams *you little shit, how dare you talk to me like that!*

"I never said he was murdered," the detective says.

"Well, surely he didn't go for a swim." *Oh fuck, I want those words back.*

"Jack, mind yourself!" my father says firmly and completely out of patience.

I do a quick inventory. First, Peter and I have done nothing wrong. Every step we made has been on the up-and-up. The painting was abandoned; Peter filed a claim with the court. We hired a detective to find relatives who could lead us to photos and paperwork. All legit. Neither one of us asked Cohen to follow Mr. Philips—that was his idea. We didn't get him killed. *I still am deeply sorry and more than a little shocked that he is dead. Scared, even. But we are not responsible.*

I give the detectives three details as politely as possible without elaborating. We went to Brooklyn, just Mr. Cohen and I—that triggers a really bad reaction from my dad. He stomps his feet and shakes his head in total frustration. "Then, we went to a diner to meet a man who was interested in purchasing the painting," I add. "Mr. Cohen waited outside. The last time either one of us saw him was earlier that day."

I leave out Kasper Greenstreet's ghost and the sinister shadows in the painting that possess it, or rather haunt it. I also offer no commentary on the possibility that Mr. Philips, who I think should be the number one suspect, may also be a sorcerer, warlock, or worse. At the very least, he is someone who practices voodoo or some other kind of black magic. *I'm not sure exactly what that fucker is, but he's definitely capable of murder.*

They drill me, asking the same questions over and over in a roundabout way. "Tell us again what was it you were looking for in Brooklyn?" *I guess these men were never interrogated by nuns.*

"Anything that could help us with the provenance of the painting." They stare at me, as does my dad. "Custody of ownership," I add.

"Yes, we know what provenance means. Did you find anything?"

"You should ask Peter that; he is the lawyer. All of this has been filed in the courts."

"We are talking about murder; Cohen didn't accidently fall in the river." My father practically screams it at me, not caring who can hear him.

The severity of that hits me on the way home. Dad gives it to me with both barrels. Well-deserved. "Brooklyn! With some guy who I don't even know."

"Dad, he was an ex-cop; he worked for us."

"Was." He looks at me with that stare only dads can give. "And he worked for Peter, who is going to get an ear full."

Peter cannot survive that. "Dad, please don't."

If my father knew about Peter chasing me with a butcher knife, he would have put Peter in Bellevue by other means.

"Well, I don't think Mr. Cohen's death has anything to do with us," I say. I'm lying but trying to lighten the tension.

"Oh, you don't? What are you and Peter, the fucking Hardy Boys?" It feels like he said that with a hint of jealousy. We walk up 2nd Avenue in silence.

When I finally reach Peter, he is not at all nervous about talking to the cops; although, he is frightened about having to come back to the city.

"Everything is moving through the courts smoothly. Hiring Mr. Cohen was all about due diligence," he says.

Peter is convinced the murderer was some rich philandering husband whose wife hired Cohen to help with a divorce case. Complete denial on his part. My instincts are in contradiction with Peter's thinking because I know Cohen's death has everything to do with Mr. Philips, but I don't want to plant that seed in his head, especially since he has convinced himself otherwise. Peter is very troubled every time he's in the city, and he will not stay overnight.

He eventually gives the detectives information so they can contact the court to see the record. The information Cohen provided us regarding the painting is documented. He also provides them with copies of the checks he paid Cohen, as well as the information on the check that Cohen never cashed. Peter also wants to speak to my dad and apologize for having me dragged into this situation. I remind him it was I who opened Pandora's box.

However, this is all before someone drops a dime on me, revealing all to my father. The police being called to Peter's apartment. The knife. His stay at Bellevue. *It is a disaster.*

My father goes ballistic. "What is wrong with you, Jack?"

"I fell on my head… remember?"

My father looks at me like he wants to beat the shit out of me. Watching Dad struggle to control himself is a struggle for me, too, because I feel like I'm putting him through it. Although, that is not my intention.

"Did I do something to you?"

"What?"

"It's a simple question, Jack, because I don't understand the lying, the disrespectful attitude. Surely I must have done something to you that, in my apparent feebleness as a parent, I am unaware of."

"You just don't understand, Dad."

"Educate me."

"About what?"

"About the police being called to Peter's apartment with a report stating he was chasing you with a knife. That he ended up in Bellevue in the psych ward, which you hid from me. First, the psychic, then the Tarot cards. What exactly is your relationship with Peter? Why would he chase you with a knife?"

My head is splitting open. I try to manage the throbbing and building migraine without using it as an excuse. We stand there in silence. *It's my fault, I fear.* There was a time when Dad and I were never like this, never at a loss for words.

"I didn't forget to tell you. It was… it was deliberate, and it was wrong. The police had it wrong, though," I say softly. *Here I go, Jack the liar, but what am I to do?* You experience this shit and then have to explain it to someone. "He wasn't chasing me. I thought Peter was going to cut his wrists."

There is good and evil, white magic and black magic, angels and demons. *It's all true because I've encountered all of these things personally. So, what I just said, I will not judge myself for, because I love my father and I love Peter.*

"Okay." *Okay?* "Don't lie to me anymore, Jack. I'm on your side."

This makes me feel incredibly guilty. I know he's on my side. I also know I will lie to him again.

Peter and I give the detectives everything we can on Mr. Philips, which honestly is not much. He seemed to materialize from nowhere and has disappeared the same way. We share his number and the diner where we met to discuss the painting. We tell the detectives about Susan's cousin in Brooklyn and how Mr. Philips went out to see her just before Cohen and I. That is all we have on him. That is all we know.

They cannot locate Mr. Philips; it seems he vanished too. His telephone number has been disconnected, which was a telephone service anyway so there was never an address attached to it. According to the detectives, who will not tell me much of anything, the diner is closed. There is nothing, not a trace. *How can you just disappear?*

I take it upon myself to visit the diner. *It's not that I don't believe the detectives, it's just all so strange… but maybe not strange at all.*

It's closed. As I walk around the property, the diner appears to have been closed for years. *How could that be possible? I was just there!* I check the doors, which are locked. There is blackout paper on the windows, so trying to peer in is useless. On my second trip around the exterior, I find a bathroom window that is slightly open. It's too high for me, so I need a boost to climb into the window. I find some wooden crates stacked by the dumpster and use them as a ladder.

It's totally dark inside the diner. I leave the bathroom window wide open for a little light. *Not sure what I am looking to find—a sacrifice? A den of witches sitting around a candle, putting spells on people in the dark?* Feeling my way through the darkness like a blind man, I make my way to the front door. It's locked and needs a key to open it. The glass door is covered in blackout paper, which I peel away, bringing light into the room. I do the same with the windows. Now at least I can move about the diner to get a better view. The kitchen is empty and dirty. There is no cooking equipment. I open cabinets one by one; all of them are bare. I walk in front of a quietly humming freezer.

As soon as I place my hand on the handle, the murmurs begin. Soft chanting voices. I release the handle and turn back to the main dining area to have a look. Silence. No one there. Focusing back on the freezer, I grab the handle. Once again, there is a low murmur. This time, I'm patient. It gets louder.

DETECTIVE COHEN AND PHILIPS

Cohen watches as Jack and Peter walk to the table so he can get a good look at Philips. He stays outside, waiting to follow him, smoking a cigarette, expecting Philips to come out of the front entrance of the diner. But Mr. Philips leaves through the kitchen. Peter and Jack stay seated at the table until he's gone. There is an echo in the diner. The place is infested with witches, warlocks, and sorcerers and not the good kind. Peter starts to speak, but I motion for him to be quiet.

He is caught off guard when Philips practically runs into him coming out the back door.

Philips stops and stares at Cohen as if he is reading him, which he is, but Cohen is unaware of it.

"Are you looking for me?" Philips asks firmly.

Cohen has been a cop, a private detective, and an addict. He prides himself with his ability to assess people rather quickly, but his read on this guy comes up empty. Well, not exactly empty. It is as if Philips has stepped into a photo in which he doesn't belong.

"Um, yes," Cohen says, motioning for Philips to walk with him. He doesn't move.

"Are you with them?" Philips asks.

The man is cutting right to the chase. Cohen is not sure if he likes this, but it might make doing business easier. "Yes—and no," Cohen says.

"What does that mean?"

Again, Cohen motions for Philips to come and walk with him. Still, he does not move. "I need to talk to you without them seeing us."

They walk along the docks without a word until they are out of view from the diner. "Explain," Philips says.

"I'm a private eye."

"And?"

"And I am technically working for Peter Cairo. I know you are interested in the painting."

Philips shrugs his shoulders. "So?"

"He won't sell it, will he?" Cohen asks.

"You tell me."

Cohen smiles, but the smile leaves his face when he sees the intensity in Philips' eyes. Not intense exactly… more like evil.

"No. He won't sell it," Cohen says flatly.

"Why? I'm willing to offer him a lot of money."

Cohen pauses. This is that line you are not supposed to cross. You are not supposed to betray the people you are working for, especially when it can get someone hurt, but he's done it before as a cop. Cohen was a dirty cop with lots of problems and lots of vices, including his love of cocaine and hookers. Three divorces and a shitload of debt erased whatever moral compass he may have once had. Now he is willing to swindle Peter if it means he can land himself a huge pay day.

"It's the kid, right?" Philips says. It is more a statement than a question.

Cohen nods his head.

"He holds power over Peter. Yes?"

Again, Cohen nods.

"How?" Philip asks. Cohen raises his shoulders to indicate he doesn't know. "An invocation? A shadow-field?"

Cohen is afraid, although he is not certain why. He doesn't understand the terms Philips is using.

"You can get me this painting?" Philips says, more a demand than a question.

Cohen does not have the fortitude to walk away from money, but he realizes Philips is dangerous. "If the kid was out of the way, I could definitely get Peter to sell," Cohen suggests.

"Surely you're not suggesting that I kill the boy?" Philips says, licking his lips.

"Of course not." Cohen suddenly wants to run. He feels like a rat or mouse being trapped by a larger animal.

Philips' eyes change to the lightest blue. Cohen sees himself at his worst and feels himself shrink. "How can you get me the painting?" Philips asks. "That is the reason you're here."

"Why do you want the painting so badly?"

"That's my concern. Your concern is how to get it for me."

"The reason I ask is because you might not be able to sell it—at least not in the immediate future," Cohen says.

"Not a worry."

Cohen takes a deep breath. "I know where the painting is stored."

"Do you have the key?"

"No."

"Can you get the key?" When Cohen nods, Philips adds, "You really want to steal the painting from your own client?" Silence. It's out there; no going back now. "How much do you want?" Philips asks.

"The painting is worth at least $255,000."

"I asked you how much you want."

The sky gets ominously dark. Cohen is cold, tired, and now frightened. "Fifty thousand."

Philips reaches out and shakes Cohen's hand. Cohen feels as if there has been a physical exchange—something has been given to him that he does not want, and something has been taken away that he needs.

I let go of the handle. When I release, the images of Philips and Cohen fade away. Quickly, I put my hand back on the handle, but the source is no longer there. I realize the freezer is unplugged, and the humming has stopped. I slowly open the freezer and find a bunch of mouse carcasses. *Disgusting!*

I go through the diner top to bottom, satisfied with the vacancy of the place. I head back to the bathroom. A low hum turns into a loud breathing sound as if the walls are alive. It makes me momentarily dizzy. *Keep moving, Jack. No, this is why you are here.* I refocus, get my head on straight. The sound brings me back into the main section of the diner. I look the place over, expecting to see Philips. Nothing.

Yet, I know that I am not alone. "Show yourself," I state firmly.

I hear Philips' voice very clearly in my head: "I want that painting! I can make you very powerful."

A lie. He will not share power. "Never," I whisper.

Suddenly, a mouse scurries in from the kitchen, followed by a silver cat that pounces on it and tears it to shreds. The pure violence is unsettling, along with the sudden manifestation of both creatures. I remember Philips' words to Peter: "Afraid of a little wind, Peter? What are you, a mouse?"

Taking a breath, I look around. "Just so we're clear, I'm not a fucking mouse!"

I wait for a windstorm but get nothing. Walking back through the diner, I begin to rip the blackout paper from a window. Sunlight pours in. "Mr. Philips? Mr. Philips, can we talk?" I ask as I tear the blackout paper off all the windows. *Let there be light!* "Mr. Philips?"

Nothing. I stand in the middle of the room.

Finally, it's time to go. I use the back of the toilet to climb out the window. My legs dangle behind me as I pull my upper torso through. It is getting dark.

Abruptly, I feel the impact of a cat crashing against me, attacking my leg. "I want that painting!" echoes in surround sound in my head.

With all the force I can muster, I shake the cat off my leg and kick it into the wall. Standing on the top of the toilet, I'm ready for battle. The cat has changed color; it is now black. *Who the fuck is this guy!?* "I'll drown your ass!" I say as the cat hisses at me before running from the room.

As I climb out of the window, I notice someone has removed the crates, forcing me to jump to the ground. *You should be home doing homework instead of chasing these fucking ghouls, Jack.* But I feel compelled that this is my calling, my destiny.

COHEN AND PHILIPS

Cohen leaves Philips on the docks after they exchange telephone numbers and set a time to meet. Cohen finds an employee with drug and money problems at Chelsea Storage—where Jack had stored the painting. Cohen greases the employee's palm with a taste of the money to come and the promise of a bigger payday. Cohen needs another key to storage B21. There is the usual squawking. "It's impossible." Cohen makes him a better offer. The way around this guy's misgivings is through his drug addiction.

Philips keeps Cohen waiting. It is very late when he arrives at Chelsea Storage. Cohen's attitude gives way to Philips' presence, which is powerful, dark, sinister. Otherworldly. It throws Cohen off balance. The building is closed, but Cohen has the right tools and picks the lock. He gives Philips copies of the paperwork and shows him the newly made key to storage B21. Then, he witnesses a literal change in Philips' skin.

B21 is on the second floor. No one is in the building but Cohen and Philips. Philips' temperature has changed, too. He becomes the groom getting ready to see his bride. Cohen is aware of the significant transformation and hands Philips the key. His eyes are on fire as he slides the key into the lock, slowly turning the handle and opening the door.

The storage unit is empty.

JACK

The Cohen murder case stays cold. I spend a lot of time in the library, not doing homework, but researching shapeshifters. It's all that is on my mind after the incident with the cats at the diner and Peter's house in Hudson Valley. The wolf. The fact that Mr. Philips seems to be out of place, out of time, in the wrong movie. These incidents lead me to entertain this idea.

Shapeshifting appears throughout history, mythology, and folklore. All cultures and tribes have stories about shapeshifting. There is even a name for a person turning into a cat—an Ailuranthrope. Some people think shapeshifting can come from a totem, a spirit, sacred object, or symbol. By the Middle Ages, it was still believed sorcerers, or witches, could shapeshift. *If they could pull it off then, why not now?*

No one can locate Mr. Philips. And, he seemed to appear from nowhere. Even Kasper while alive and his ghost could not identify or find him. But the painting on the wall of Mr. Philips sent Kasper into a maelstrom of emotion. *Mr. Philips is much more powerful than I originally thought. Never underestimate your opponent.*

I find a definition of shapeshifter in an encyclopedia of religion: "Shapeshifting can be defined as an alteration in form or substance of any animate object. There seems to be no limit to the kind of objects susceptible to such alteration. Examples: plants, animals, humans, and gods." That I find tricky because I believe there is only one God, one source. Shapeshifting can be caused by an external force and can occur for good or evil, for reasons simple or profound. It is not a phenomenon restricted to unsophisticated cultures remote in history and geography. There are elements of shapeshifting in the deepest and even modern spiritual insights of Christianity, Hinduism, and Buddhism. It is found in dominant civilizations and popular modern cultures as well as in major religions.

Angels and demons? Shapeshifters?

Suddenly, the chatter in the library rises to a ridiculously high level. Looking around, I know I'm picking up on the thoughts of the librarian and patrons. Only, there are not nearly enough people here to create such high volume. While trying to stay focused amidst the chaos, I realize the voices are coming from the books. Closing my eyes, I try to equalize the sound and differentiate the words coming at me all at once.

It's overwhelming, like the first time in the subway with my father. I hone in on what the voices from the books are trying to tell me.

Peter and I get good news; he has won the case. The painting now officially belongs to him. He immediately converts that into joint ownership with me.

"Why are you doing that, Peter? It's yours," I say from a pay phone on 19th Street. My father is livid with the entire knife-wielding incident so I can't talk from home anymore. Now I use different pay phones in the city. Peter tells me to call collect, which I do on occasion.

"It's not completely altruistic, Jack," he says. "Like the tenants before me, I would never have opened that storage bin. That was you. However, more importantly, if we can't sell the painting without the other one's approval, we will stick to our word and never sell it."

I'm in agreement, but the truth is we sound bat shit crazy. Here we are, sitting on a painting worth upward of $250,000 that we are promising never to sell.

When talking with him, I'm reminded of something: the more removed Peter is from the city and the supernatural elements that engulfed his life, the better he sounds. He is practicing law again and has never been happier with his parents. Mr. Cairo still can't speak, but his writing is clear enough with his left hand that he is able to communicate his needs and wants without his old frustration. Peter and Julia both credit me with helping him through the use of the coloring books, which improved his left-hand motor skills. *I'll take it, but I'm not sure it's warranted.*

Standing alone in the phone booth, I miss the Cairos daily and deeply. *Maybe it isn't so far-fetched that I created my own family; maybe I always wanted that sort of an intact unit.* Listening to the sound of his voice, I am sure he will never move back to the city, which makes me sad. But I love them, so I must be happy for them. They are where they should be. *Me? I am where I am.*

I walk out of school one afternoon with my head down, knowing it's just a matter of time before shit hits the fan with my failing grades. I don't try to muscle through; I'm just failing, and I don't care. This is a first. Feeling for the joint in my pocket, it takes me a moment to realize the two detectives are waiting for me just outside school property.

I fake a smile. "Detectives."

"Jack."

"What's up?"

"Let's walk," Detective Gruff says as more of a command. "Is there anything you overlooked? Anything you forgot to tell us?"

I shake my head. "Like what?"

"That's what we're asking you."

"Did you find Mr. Philips?" I know they haven't, but I ask anyway.

"Not yet, but we did find out that Mr. Cohen worked on a case years ago, possibly looking for the same guy." They wait for a response, which I don't give. "Not much in his old file."

"Oh?" I say. "That's interesting."

"Yes, he was working for Kasper Greenstreet." The detective lets that resonate within me.

"Kasper Greenstreet…" I repeat. Not with a question mark, but not without one, either.

"The same Kasper Greenstreet that Mr. Cohen was helping you and Peter Cairo track down paperwork for..." Detective Gruff takes a long dramatic pause then continues, "Um… provenance."

I'd love to say *touché*, but I don't dare. "So, you think Mr. Cohen was looking for Mr. Philips years ago?" I ask.

"Maybe. Did he tell you anything?"

"You think that's what I overlooked? That he was looking for Mr. Philips on a previous case?"

"Did he tell you he worked for Kasper Greenstreet, once upon a time?"

A headache is knocking on my door, which makes me pause longer than I need to. "I don't recall if he did, or if he didn't."

"Do you think that would be important?"

"Wait. I'm confused. Which one is more important—that he may have been looking for Mr. Philips or that, once upon a time, he worked briefly for Kasper Greenstreet?" I ask.

"Let me buy you an ice cream," Detective Gruff says as we get to the corner. *I can shake them off here and say I need to go home, but having friends on the police force is always a good idea. Right?*

"I can't. Sorry. I'm lactose intolerant."

"Are you trying to piss me off?" Detective Gruff is losing his patience.

"No, you can buy me a cup of tea. Really, I don't eat ice cream."

Inside, they order coffee while I order tea. "Both—that he was maybe looking for Mr. Philips and that he worked for Kasper Greenstreet," Detective Gruff picks up where he left off. He does ninety-eight percent of the talking.

"If he did tell us that he worked for Kasper Greenstreet—and I'm not sure he told us that—at the time, it wasn't important to me," I tell him.

"Why?"

"Kasper Greenstreet was dead. As for Mr. Philips, if the old file says he was looking for Mr. Philips previously, then it could be important now because of the circumstances. But, again, at the time, we were just looking for Susan Michaels' cousin and paperwork to support Peter's case."

He turns the entirety of his sizeable body to face me. It looks like a posture of intimidation, but I'm not intimidated. "So, you and Peter did not deliberately leave this information out?"

"No. Does the file say he was looking for Mr. Philips? Our Mr. Philips? Same number? Did it give a reason?"

"You should practice law, Jack," the easygoing detective says. "I bet you are the smartest kid in your class." *Is he being sarcastic? He appears to be genuine, but you can't tell with adults sometimes. They like to patronize.*

"Really? Me?"

"You are a very sharp kid," says Detective Gruff, "but you don't have to be such a wise ass."

"Well, I hate to disappoint you, fellows, but I'm flunking most of my classes at the moment." They both seem genuinely surprised. "Did it say why Kasper Greenstreet hired him?"

"A man by the name of Philip tried to kill him. Beat him up pretty bad."

That's the one. "Philip? Or Mr. Philips?" I ask.

"Only the first name, but damn coincidental, don't you think?"

"God's way of talking to you," I reply nonchalantly.

"What?" asks the easygoing detective.

"A coincidence. It's God's way of talking to you. At least that's my take on it."

"Jack, you know the woman you met in Brooklyn, the cousin, the one with the boxes in the basement?" the easygoing detective asks.

"Yes. Was she able to help you?"

"She seems to have disappeared."

"What?"

"Last time a neighbor saw her, she was heading into the basement. No one has seen her since."

"Did she go visit a relative?" I ask, genuinely concerned.

The easygoing detective shakes his head. "The apartment did not look like anyone was planning on going anywhere. She had lunch waiting for her on the table."

Outside the coffee shop, the detectives urge me to go home and study. They give me their business cards. "Call us anytime you need to, kid."

My mind is racing. *I guess I'll be heading out to Brooklyn.*

At dinner, I break it to my father that it isn't working out for me at Xavier. "You should expect a phone call from the dean," I say. Surprisingly, he doesn't fight with me or yell, but his disappointment is written all over his face.

Later, I can't sleep. All I do is toss and turn. No amount of meditation or yoga is going to help me sleep.

After I make sure my dad is out for the count, I slide out the kitchen window, down the fire escape, and into the small yard behind our tenement. My first stop is Epiphany School and the Gramercy Terrace apartments. When I arrive, I see no lights from apartment 3C. There is a new tenant in the apartment. I'm sure things are different now that Kasper vacated the premises—no hauntings, no shadows, no sleepless nights.

I stand in front of Epiphany and look at the window of my previous classroom. The birds and their attack come to mind, as well as Sister Elizabeth. Now I understand the reason I picked up on the breast situation: Sister has a lump in one of them, a cancerous lump. *Is this what I needed to understand?* I hold the triangle that hangs from my neck, the one Mr. David gave me. *Do I tell her? Should I tell her?*

From 22nd Street, I head to the 23rd Street subway, where my first encounter with the supernatural happened. The memory of the ghost of that woman throwing herself in front of the train over and over again comes to mind. There is one person waiting on the platform. He looks me over and checks his watch. *Yup, it's late for me to be out wandering by myself,* but I wander anyway. I find myself in front of the site where the old boarding house stood. Looks like construction has restarted. I press my hands on a board, hoping for… *what? To pick up some old energy? To understand why my life changed on this site?* No clarity or answers come.

I make the short subway trip, walk home, unlock the door, and tiptoe into the apartment. My dad is still asleep. As I get ready for bed, I wonder *are we really awake when we think we're dreaming? Or am I dreaming now?*

I sit at the table in the boarding house kitchen. It is nothing like the night when I fell through the floor and almost died here. My injured body does not lie between the world of the living and the dead. No one else is sitting at the table. There are no shadows or demons crawling around me. It is just the nun and I. Her back is to me.

She makes us tea in the kitchen. "You are back?" she asks without turning around.

"Yes."

"Tea?" She does not wait for my answer and pours us each a cup of tea from a scarlet red kettle.

When she turns to face me, I can see she is luminous, like she has swallowed the sun. It radiates from her, lighting and warming the space around us.

Placing the tea down in front of me, she speaks. "May I ask why?"

I'm surprised by the question, even a bit hurt. It makes me sit up and back away, like a wounded child. "Do you not want me to come here?"

The nun places her cup on the table and sits so that we are facing one another. The warmth from her light feels comforting on my face.

She sips her tea and looks at me intently. "It's always up to you."

That's not the answer I want. I wait. *Looking at her for what? Affection? I want her to want me to come, I want her approval, her love.* "But do you not want me to come?" No answer. "I mean I know I can always find you here. Right?"

"Why? Because this is where we met?" she asks.

"Yes."

Drinking her tea is like drinking air. That doesn't make sense, but it does to me.

She is waiting on me. Her eyes are patient; her body relaxed. She knows I am here for a specific reason. "This is just a dream? Right?"

"Does that matter?" she asks.

"I want it to be real."

She smiles at me. *In a motherly way?* "Then it's real."

"Real… okay. I came here because Sister Elizabeth, my last teacher at Epiphany, a nun like you…" She nods. "She has three breasts," I blurt out.

The nun looks at me and smiles. "Did you come here to ask me if all nuns have three breasts?"

Wow, she's being funny. Unexpected. It makes me feel calm and safe. Alive. "No, of course not. It's just that she has a lump in one of them." She nods her head, as if to say *I see.* "I'm not sure it's malignant."

There is a powerful connection between us now. She has saved me from death the first time and now I need her help again to save me from... what? Mr. Philips? The painting? Myself?

I need her strength and her wisdom. We drink our tea in silence. It is not an awkward silence but heartfelt and soothing. I wonder if her tea tastes like air too.

"Earth," she finally says.

"What?" Why does it still surprise me that we do not need words. Everything between us is and always has been telepathic.

Raising her cup. "My tea—it tastes like earth."

"May I taste it?" I ask.

She pushes her cup towards me on the table. "Sure, but it will taste like air to you."

I let that sit with me, not reaching for her cup. "Oh, I see, I think I get it."

The nun smiles. "So, you have a question."

"Yes. Should I tell Sister Elizabeth?"

The nun sips her tea. She is much younger than I originally thought. Her eyes are hazel. Gentle. *She would have been a marvelous mother.* "If I may ask, how did you die?"

"I was murdered." She speaks with no anger or vengeance. I remember that from the article Peter showed me of a nun's bones being found during the excavation.

"Do you know who killed you?" I ask.

"Yes, but none of that matters now."

"Why?"

She looks at me, curious about my questioning. "Why doesn't it matter? Or why did he kill me?"

"Both, I guess."

"Because I have forgiven him. He was ill, and he thought I was a witch."

I look down, then back up, meeting her eyes. They are kind, warm. "But you weren't?"

"Heavens, no. He thought my use of holistic remedies were potions. That I wanted to poison him."

I play with my teacup, hoping I haven't offended her. "What should I do about Sister Elizabeth?"

She folds her hands and seems to be weighing the answer. "What can you do?"

"I could tell her."

She shrugs her shoulders. "So, tell her."

"Well, it's not that easy."

"It never is…"

"Last year, things happened. Very weird events. I think Sister Elizabeth thought I created, or rather, caused them."

She takes her cup and brings it to the sink. When she returns to the table, she stays standing, looking at me. *Challenging me?* But I do not feel threatened or put upon.

"What does any of that have to do with telling her about her cancer?" the nun asks.

"I'm afraid she will react badly, that she'll think I'm some kind of psychic, occultist, or even a witch."

She gives me a reassuring smile. "But you're not a witch or an occultist."

"No, of course not. I'm just a boy."

She tilts her head and looks into my soul. "We both know that you are not just a boy, Jack."

My eyes tear up. *At last, I feel understood for the first time since I woke up in the hospital as just a boy, utterly confused.*

"And why should it matter what someone thinks?" She asks before I can explore those feelings with her. "You know it's not true; your intent is pure. If you are coming from a place of love, then the intention is pure."

"Yes." I nod.

She looks up disturbed. "Did you bring him?" she asks.

"Who?"

I follow her eyes as she looks outside of the kitchen and into the darkness. There, with a soft light on his face, is Mr. Philips. The idea of him being here shocks me.

"I must have because it's my dream, correct?" I ask.

Her attention changes from Mr. Philips back to me. "So, you are dreaming?"

"I'm not sure. Either way, it must be me who brought him. Unless you know him... do you?"

She shakes her head watching him. She is not afraid exactly, but uneasy.

We remain silent for a moment. Then I ask, "Is he dead or alive?"

"He just is," she says.

"I don't understand. He is what?"

"He is not like you or like me. He is somewhere in the in-between. In a liminal zone. He occupies space between two worlds. Not living or dead as we know it. He just is..."

I look at the nun and then at Mr. Philips, who fades into the darkness.

"Don't we have to be one or the other? Dead or alive?"

She doesn't answer immediately. She makes me wait. I guess so that I will think about my own question. Finally, she says, "Dead. Alive. Those are just words we create to try and explain things that we don't fully understand when we are having a human experience."

"But you're dead, and I'm alive? Right?"

The nun shrugs her shoulders. "Yet, here we are, talking to one another and having tea," she says.

This makes me feel very funny, not "ha, ha" funny, either. Oddly funny. "Am I dead now?" I ask, barely able to utter the words.

"There is no dead, no living—those are only terms," she replies. "I told you there just is."

My father wakes me, pulling me back to my physical reality as a fifteen-year-old high school student. Getting me up for school seems ridiculous since I know they are going to expel me. I tell him that.

"Well," he says, "you'll go until they actually do it. Right now, it's all in your head."

No, Dad. What's in my head is that there is no dead, no living—there just is...

Dad sets a bowl of oatmeal on the table for me and heads out the door, on his way to work. "Do your best!" he yells.

Putting all my energy and effort into school seems futile, but I decide to try. I make it through the day, but when it's over, I can't get out of the building fast enough. The butterflies cannot escape my stomach, so they make themselves at home. Walking toward Epiphany, I'm counting on Sister Elizabeth to be in the classroom, as she always is on Tuesday afternoon. I quickly move past the front office and hit the stairs two at a time, hoping no one sees or tries to stop me. *I don't want a scene.* My fear is that if I don't do this now, if I don't tell her today, I never will.

The door to the classroom is open, but I knock anyway, not wanting to startle her. Sister Elizabeth looks up from her desk. She cannot conceal her dismay—even trepidation—at the sight of me.

"Mr. Kelly?"

"Good afternoon, Sister, please forgive my interruption."

She motions for me to come in. "Sit if you like." No matter how cordial we try to be, there is too much water under the bridge, as they say. The uneasiness between us is palpable so I decide to cut to the chase.

"Sister Elizabeth, I've been praying about this for a really long time. And, well... as you know, we are taught that God listens, answers..." *I'm not sure if I sound crazy, but I can't stop or I will never say it.* "If I may say, after much prayer, I feel the need—the calling really—to tell you that I believe you need to see a doctor regarding a mass or lump in one of your breasts. I think it it's cancerous."

My stomach feels like it's risen to my esophagus, butterflies and all; I may vomit right here on the floor. The need to curse is pulsating on my tongue like the tic of a person with Tourette syndrome, ready to explode.

Sister doesn't speak. Instead, she stares at me like I've lost my fucking mind. Her humiliation rising like a volcano ready to erupt. I've mortified her in my feeble attempt to warn her, to help her.

"God, Mr. Kelly? God told you to come here and tell me this?" Sister asks incredulously, her head shaking gently side to side. Her eyes studying me. I feel her displeasure.

I step back, planning my escape route.

"Prayer, God, intuition." I'm mumbling now. *This is a mistake.*

"Intuition?" Her discomfort is palpable. Her eyes are filling up with tears. *Jack, what have you done?*

We stare at each other. Both of us lost in who we are and who we are not. Sister takes a moment to compose herself.

Finally, she says. "I'll take it into consideration, Mr. Kelly." Then after a long pause, she says firmly, "You may go."

"You may go?" Wow, lady, I just told you that you may have cancer. Do you know how hard that was? I leave the room and run down the stairs; I can't get out of the building fast enough. *Stupid. My decision to see her was stupid.* Sister Elizabeth does not see me as helping; she sees me as something wicked. One thing for sure, I know which nun, of the two that I have visited in the last twenty-four hours, I am guided by. "You may go" rings loudly in my head.

My intent was pure; of that, I am certain.

My next stop is Brooklyn. I can't find the address and certainly can't get it from Cohen. I also decide not to call Peter. He seems to withdraw every time we have a conversation or when our conversation leads to a new piece of information regarding the painting, Kasper Greenstreet, Mr. Philips, or Cohen. I'm pretty sure I can find the building where Susan Michaels' cousin, Mrs. Walsh, lives from memory. While on my way, I keep thinking about how disappointed I am with Sister Elizabeth's reaction. The least I was hoping for was "Okay, I'll look into it."

Then, a reminder comes to me. *Remember, Jack, be of service without being attached to its results. That is something I need to live by because, let's face it, many of the results have not been good.*

SISTER ELIZABETH

What in God's name is with this kid… as if Jack Kelly didn't bring enough crazy, supernatural events to my life last school year?

Sister Elizabeth waits for Jack to leave her classroom and counts to ten before walking into the hall to make sure he is not lurking about. She prays aloud, "Forgive me, Father, but that child upsets me." The sound of Jack running down the stairs and jumping to the landing reassures her that he is gone. Her body shakes. *He must have brought back some evil with him.* All she feels she can do is pray for Jack Kelly.

The school's front doors shut, the sound pulling her back into the classroom. She looks out the window to see him on the sidewalk. There he is, walking toward 3rd Avenue. The feelings he creates within her bring such shame. She does not like the boy. *There is something wicked in him. These feelings, and what he carries inside, cannot possibly come from God!*

Sister Elizabeth shuts the window and looks across the street at the old apartment of Peter Cairo. News of him moving out of the city this summer was whispered about through the parish. It is common knowledge in the convent. *Thank God he is gone. He is another one carrying the devil's influence. He had that full mental breakdown I witnessed; that may be his excuse.* However, she is sure that whatever was going on in that apartment was unholy. It was horrifying seeing Peter Cairo, a grown man, chase Jack around the apartment, wielding a knife. Then Jack lied to Father Keenan, saying it didn't happen. She witnessed it with her own two eyes. *Shameful.*

What was Peter Cairo doing with Jack that would cause him to chase him with a knife? The whole episode still made her feel uneasy.

Another question crossed her mind. *What type of child, or teenager, comes to tell a nun at a religious school that he thinks she has a mass on one of her breasts? Was that some kind of slight or code, wanting me to know that he is aware of my three breasts? How could he know that? Ridiculous.* Yet, there was something about his delivery: "One of your breasts." Like he was aware that there were more than two…

She buries her face in her hands, trying to shut out the world, his comment bringing her shame front and center. *Is this his way of getting back at me? To punish me for how I disciplined him last year after the bird and train incidents? "Incidents" do not describe it well at all—it was demonic!* She thought she was done with Jack Kelly. She decides she should call his father; it's unseemly for a boy to talk to a nun about her breasts. Or to any woman, for that matter.

She has to be on her way. After shutting her binder and lesson plan, she walks slowly down the stairs. The walls fill up with shadows, mocking her, accusing her, shaming her. *I am, after all, a sinner.*

She walks into the convent. Her habit suddenly feels like it weighs a ton so she walks straight to her living quarters and removes it. She then peels off her undergarments until she stands naked. She touches her breasts one at a time; something she has not done since… *the pleasure of my body when I was with Mr. Dillon.*

She shakes off that memory and gives herself a full breast self-exam. On the right breast, there it is—a lump. She checks it over and over again. She feels the lump every time. *When did this happen? Why?*

What Jack said was true.

Once again, her body has betrayed her. She falls into a heap on the floor and begins sobbing.

BROOKLYN

My head is not in the game; I am still upset over Sister Elizabeth. I have shamed her, and in doing so, I feel shame myself. I get off at the wrong stop but manage to jump back on the train before the doors close. While walking into Mrs. Walsh's building, I try to develop a plan. *What am I looking for that the detectives were unable to find?* I'm hoping my intuition tells me.

I knock on her door, but I don't expect anyone to answer. I am not disappointed. After looking around the hallway for prying eyes, I turn the knob; it's locked. Down the hall, the sound of an apartment door opening gets my attention. It's the door for 1A. Out steps the little boy I met the last time I was here.

"Hey," I say as he moves farther into the hallway. "I'm looking for Mrs. Walsh."

He walks a little closer to me. "She's not home."

"What's your name?"

"Michael."

I smile at him. "Oh, like Michael the Archangel?"

"I don't know who that is," Michael says flatly, emotionlessly.

"He's the most powerful angel of them all."

Michael stops in the middle of the hall, watching me. *There is something strange about him, for sure, but I'll bet that's what people say about me.*

"Do you know where she is?" I ask.

He points toward the door of the basement. I walk to the basement door and turn the knob; it's locked. "When did she go down there?" I ask.

Michael shrugs his shoulders.

"Was it today?"

He shakes his head.

"How do you know she's still down there?" I ask.

"I hear the noises at night."

"Noises?"

"Yes." Michael holds his ears.

"The noises are loud?" He nods. I take a deep breath, then ask, "Do you only hear noises at night?"

"Yes, that's when he comes!" Michael says it excitedly, fearfully.

"Who is 'he?'"

Michael's eyes pop. He spreads his hands out, in a menacing way, his arms fully extended, imitating… what? A giant? A monster? He is a peculiar little boy, but the way he immediately stretched his arms out when I asked causes me to believe him.

"Do you have a key?" I ask.

Michael turns and walks back into his apartment. As I stand in the hall, waiting for him, my entire body pulsates. *Is this a warning?* I hold the triangle around my neck and recite the words the man in Turkey used when he sold it to Mr. David: "The infinite power and protection of the Trinity!"

The boy comes back out of his apartment holding a key. He hands it to me. Immediately, I try the lock on the basement door. It doesn't work. I try again, as if by willpower, the lock will turn. No luck.

Michael pulls on my shirt. "It doesn't work," I say, stating the obvious.

"No."

He points to the apartment door. He takes the key out of my hand and unlocks Mrs. Walsh's apartment door but doesn't open it. He turns to me and stares.

"She's not in there," I say. "You said she was in the basement."

"She has the key."

Now I get it. "The basement key is inside her apartment?"

"Yes."

I hear high heels hitting the tiled hallway. The steps stop me from entering Mr. Walsh's apartment. I slide the key out of the lock and put it in my pocket.

"Michael," his mother says firmly in the hallway as she struggles with two grocery bags. She eyes me suspiciously.

Michael walks to his mother. She hands him one of the bags, which he promptly takes into the apartment.

"Who are you?" his mother asks sternly.

"I met your son before when Mr. Cohen and I had tea with Mrs. Walsh," I say, hoping to alleviate her fears. I walk closer to her, so she can see how young I am. I don't want her to feel threatened. "Jack Kelly."

A moment later, Michael returns to the hall from the apartment. "Mrs. Walsh was helping us with paperwork from her cousin's estate," I tell his mother.

She ponders for a moment, then her eyes soften, recalling our last visit. "Oh yeah, I sort of remember her saying something about that." Her posture eases a bit.

"Your son told me that Mrs. Walsh was in the basement," I say.

Her demeanor changes drastically; her body tightens, her eyes widen. She stands firm. It is a fight or flight stance, and she has decided to fight. "Oh, he did? What else did he tell you?"

"Just that Mrs. Walsh was down in the basement. Oh, and something about loud noises."

She stands in front of Michael in a protective manner. *Something isn't right.* "Did I say something wrong?"

"Michael is autistic." She says, but she is thinking *you're a liar.*

"Artistic?" I repeat incorrectly, thinking she means like an artist. "How cool to be a child artist and to know it at such a young age. It must be what makes him so sensitive."

"No. Autistic."

I shake my head. "Oh, I thought you said artistic. Autistic—I don't know what that is."

"Well, it's a lot of things. A wide umbrella. Each child can be very different. There are things we understand about Michael, and things we are still discovering. For one, he's nonverbal..."

It takes me a moment to get my brain around the word. "Nonverbal?"

"He doesn't talk."

Oh, Jesus. Lady, that child was clearly talking to me.

Michael steps to her side. "I talk; she just can't hear me," he says.

How do I recover from this? "Do you hear loud noises at night?" I ask Michael.

She looks down at her son as he covers his ears with his hands. "The noise bothers him. He's very sensitive to noise. Unfortunately, the building has rats," she says.

I stand there like a bobblehead doll on the dashboard of a car, nodding continuously. Finally, I ask, "Have you seen Mrs. Walsh?"

"No one has seen Mrs. Walsh for days," she says. "We saw her go down to the basement a couple of days ago. The police have already been here to check it out. No one has seen her since."

I bend down and look into Michael's eyes. "Thank you."

"I'm going to make dinner. Let's go, Michael." They walk back into their apartment.

"Nice meeting you," I call after her. I count six 'Mississippi's' in the hallway before walking backward to Mrs. Walsh's apartment and sliding inside, all the while thinking *you keep going to places you feel you must go but clearly should not be.*

Inside the apartment, I get a better understanding of what the detectives were talking about. It doesn't look like she was planning on going anywhere. *Why isn't this roped off as a crime scene?* Probably because there really hasn't been a crime, at least that anyone knows about. I pull the nicer detective's business card from my pocket and consider calling him. But I need to look around first and get into that basement.

I start with junk drawers. Everyone has a junk drawer. I check kitchen drawers and cabinets for the keys to the basement. That's where Dad and I keep everything. Not Mrs. Walsh, though. Everything about this apartment is so neat, so organized. I look at the walls, scanning, my eyes finally moving between the kitchen and the living room. There they are, hanging on a hook: the keys. They all appear to be keys to apartments, which make senses, since she is the super of the building. All the keys are of uniform design, but one appears to be a skeleton key.

After removing the keys, I walk to the door and open it a crack. After making sure there is no one in the hall, I quietly make my way out of the apartment. The skeleton key clearly is not the correct key for this door. One by one, I try all of the others; none work.

There must be another entrance. I go back into the apartment and put all the keys back, except the skeleton key.

It is beginning to get dark when I explore the outside of the building. I find a small set of stairs that lead down to the basement's exterior door. I pull out the skeleton key, and it fits!

I try opening the door, but something is blocking it. After a bit of a struggle, I open the door enough to squeeze in. I quickly realize that the items blocking the door are the boxes that Cohen and I went through. I move further into the basement, which is dark and musty. The thought of rats climbing around grosses me out. Carefully, I feel my way in the dark for the staircase. Crawling up the stairs, I am able to find and turn on the basement light.

I unlock the basement door and step out into the hall just to clear my head.

After looking around from the top of the stairs, I head back into the basement, closing the door gently behind me. *What am I looking for? Why am I here? As if my life couldn't get any stranger, it just did today. I'm hearing a mute boy talk.* I shake that off and begin to assess the place. Mrs. Walsh can't be here. The basement is congested with lots of bullshit—boxes, paint cans, an old piano. In the rear of the basement, behind the stairs, an old canvas covers a bunch of items. I look at the boxes again; it is clear that someone has gone through them. I find the box holding the Polaroids of the *Duality* exhibit. I took all of the Polaroids of Kasper's self-portrait with the shadows. They are sitting in Peter's P.O. Box. These photos are scattered, some of them missing. I have a good memory, and there were five Polaroid photos of each painting, just like Kasper's self-portrait. Not anymore.

I rummage through the boxes and find some of the bills of sale, all the while thinking *who else would want these besides me?* Last time I was here, I had asked Cohen, but he said we weren't here for bills of sale, so I left them. Now, after flipping through them, I put them all back inside the envelope and place them outside the basement door, behind a garbage can. I'll take them with me later. They may be useful.

Above, I hear the basement door squeak open. Someone is walking down the stairs.

"Are you down there?" It's Michael.

I walk to the staircase, see him, and motion for him to come down. "Where is your mother?" I ask.

"Cooking. Talking on the phone."

"How come I can hear you?" I ask. Michael shrugs his shoulders. "Can anyone else hear you?"

"Mrs. Walsh."

I nod. "She's not down here," I say.

Michael keeps nodding. "Yes. Yes. Yes," he says, flapping his hands like he is a bird getting ready for takeoff.

"Okay, calm down. Look with me."

Michael and I continue the search of the basement. I come across a sledgehammer; I pick it up and lay it on the stairs. Mrs. Walsh is not here. If she were, we would be hit with the awful smell of her decomposing body. Of course, I don't say that to the little boy. Behind the stairs, I pull the canvas off and toss it onto the floor. The canvas had been covering large and small canning jars, which are lined up in crates. Some are empty, while some are filled with fruit and others with tomatoes. Several very large jars stand against the back wall, jars three feet in height, maybe larger. They are labeled, so it is impossible to see what's in them. Climbing over the smaller jars, I make my way to them. I turn the first jar around. It looks like pickles but has a very weird smell. I clear the smaller jars out of the way so I am better able to get a handle on the bigger jars. The next jar appears to have peaches, but it does not look appetizing.

"It's getting dark," Michael says, an urgency in his voice.

I grab the last jar, struggling to turn it around.

Michael screams. A high-pitched, ear-popping shriek like a wounded animal.

"Oh my God! Oh my God! Holy fucking shit!" I scream aloud, hardly recognizing the sound of my own voice.

Mrs. Walsh is stuffed in the third tall jar. She looks like a medical specimen.

I look over my shoulder at Michael. He is in shock and will not stop his high-pitched screaming. It is creating havoc in my brain to add to the fact I am already freaking the fuck out. *What are you doing, Jack? What is this?*

"He's going to come! He's going to come!" Michael yells between his high-pitched screams.

"Who? Who's coming?"

I bring myself to look at the jar. Mrs. Walsh is curled into a fetal position in some kind of liquid. Her eyes are closed, and strands of hair float by her face like kelp at the bottom of the ocean.

"Oh no, oh no!" Michael starts to give a play-by-play of his emotions between his high-pitched screams, which continue interfering with my thoughts. "Get her out! Get her out!" he screams.

I'm too stunned to do that; clearly, she's dead. *What the fuck am I going to do with her?*

"It's here! It's here!"

I look around frantically, trying to see what he sees. I don't see anything. *The kid is making me a fucking nervous wreck! I need to get him out of the basement, fast, so I can develop a plan.*

I hand him the detective's business card. "Have your mother call this number. Now. Tell the detective where I am! Go!"

He doesn't move. "It's here! It's here!" More high-pitched screams. He stands, pointing.

A rat crawls out of a crack in the wall. *Is this what he's freaking out about? Is this what he thinks is the monster?*

I look back at the jar just as Mrs. Walsh's eyes pop open. "Ohhh, fuck!" I fall backward. *Now it's my turn to scream! She's alive? That's not possible!*

Inside the jar, though, I clearly see Mrs. Walsh mouthing, "Help!"

I try to pick up the jar, but it's too heavy. "Michael, help me!" I say, suddenly starting to panic.

He stands frozen on the staircase. I'm going to have to do this myself. As I begin to roll the jar along the concrete floor, I lose control. It rolls away from me, bouncing off the staircase. Finally, I grab the top of the jar and try to open it. It won't turn. *How the fuck can I get her out of that small opening, anyway?*

Michael has stopped screaming. Now he is pointing; his eyes wide with fear.

I follow his eyes. "Holy Mother of God! What the fuck!" I scream aloud.

The rat is contorting, its frame pulling apart and reforming into some prehistoric…I don't even know what… but some kind of prehistoric fucking animal. This happens as I'm trying to figure out what to do with the jar—*lift it and run?* I pick up the sledgehammer and decide to smash the glass in the hope of setting her free. *A mistake? We'll soon find out.*

Back in the corner, the rat-creature keeps growing, now breaking away from whatever body it has metamorphosed into, reforming again, beginning to metamorphose into something else.

I smash the jar. Mrs. Walsh tumbles out, and I get her onto the canvas cloth. She looks like a gigantic embryo; there is a smell—a sweet smell, but overly sweet—of medicine in the liquid. *Amniotic fluid? Some sorcerer's potion? I really have no idea.* It is all around her; she is slippery and gross to the touch.

Michael lets out another high-pitched scream.

I turn around. The creature is now substantially taller than I am. It is large, nasty, and angry!

I grab Michael and rush him up the stairs to get out of the basement. "Call the name on the card! Tell him I need help!"

Before we make it to the top of the stairs, though, the creature swings its long spiny tail, taking my legs out, as well as breaking several steps in the middle of the staircase. *Fuck, Jack, this is the real demon!* It is already making everything else I've experienced seem like child's play.

The creature flicks its tail at us again. This time, I slam it with the sledgehammer. Which only makes it angrier. "Go, Michael!" I push Michael out the door and into the hallway. "Call for help!"

I turn my attention back to the creature and look at it more closely. It appears to be a Cyclops with a tail. It is more than eight feet tall, maybe as tall as ten feet. Its singular eye sits high in the middle of its forehead—what Mr. David and his mystic friends call the "Third Eye."

The creature grabs my ankle and drags me back to the bottom of the stairs. While bouncing along the staircase, I snatch one of the broken steps and smash it across its head. That stops him for the moment I need to make my escape. It pursues me around the basement, crashing into things, knocking them down, destroying everything in its way.

A flash comes to me: that day in the diner, when the cat tore the mouse to bits. All those dead mice in the freezer. *I am the mouse! I better find a hole I can hide in!*

I hide behind the staircase and watch the creature as it searches for me. I reach around, trying to grab the sledgehammer again. *Jack, this may be the hill you die on. You'd better go out swinging!*

Then it spots me. I club its foot with the sledgehammer. It reaches through the stairs and grabs me by the shirt, then slams my body against the back of the staircase. I hear the crunch of one of my ribs breaking; it takes my breath away. The creature slams me again and again until I've dropped the sledgehammer.

I hang there without much fight or breath left in me; my face caught between two stairs. I reach for the triangle around my neck.

The monster and I look at each other face-to-face, separated by a few inches and broken stairs. I peer into its eye. It is the exact color, with the exact mirroring effect, as I noticed in Philips' eyes. This is all unbelievable. I know he is a shapeshifter, a sorcerer, but this creature, how can it be? What kind of shapeshifting, wizardly shit has he created? Again, his mirroring reflects the image of a warrior back to me.

That gives me instant strength and inspiration. Tearing the medallion from my neck, I plunge one of the triangle points directly into the Cyclops' eye. With all my might, I rip the eye from its socket. The Cyclops loses its grip on me, and I crash to the floor, next to Mrs. Walsh. Now blinded, the creature stumbles around the basement, recklessly bringing everything down in its way and making a horrible yell as it continues swinging wildly.

I feel like we're in the battle of David and Goliath. I crawl along the floor, pick up the sledgehammer, and go to work on him. First, I take out his right knee, then the left. The creature falls but not before landing a lucky slap that sends me flying across the basement.

As I lay on the floor, catching my breath, the Cyclops goes into full retrograde, reverse metamorphosis, turning itself back into the same rat that entered through the crack in the basement and started all of this. Now it is bloodied, with one eye missing.

I quickly get to my knees and crawl along the floor, grabbing a jar and throwing it. I miss my target, and the jar splatters on the wall. The rat bounces around, trying to find its hole. I pick up another jar and fire it across the room. I hit the rat this time, but it still slips inside the wall.

After taking a deep breath, I return to Mrs. Walsh. Her body begins to slowly open, like an accordion that hasn't been played in a very long time. I see my triangle on the floor near the rat hole. I crawl to it, grab it, and put it in my pocket. Fearing some force will drag me into the hole, I back away in a hurry, circling back behind the stairs and next to Mrs. Walsh. She stares blankly at me. Pain shoots through my body.

I close my eyes, hoping someone will come to help us.

When I open my eyes again, the basement is filled with activity, paramedics, and police. It is pandemonium. All the cops and ambulance medics have the same reaction when they see Mrs. Walsh and her crunched up form. "Is she dead?" one asks, spooked. When she opens her eyes, they are alarmed. The woman is clearly catatonic. She can't speak. They try to take vitals. Occasionally, she vomits up some of the amniotic fluid in which she was floating. They rush her out of the building into a waiting ambulance. The look on seasoned responders' faces when they see the damage in the basement, along with my ghostly complexion, is pretty easy to read: *What the fuck happened here?*

They immediately take my vitals and check my eyes. I look like a corpse. It is the same look anytime I have a fierce supernatural experience.

Within moments, Brooklyn police have already begun asking me questions. *Honestly, I don't know how or where to begin.* I feign confusion. How do I describe finding Mrs. Walsh in a jar? A rat turning into a Cyclops? Any answer I give will probably earn me a one-way ticket to Bellevue or another psych ward. *No thank you!*

I notice that the inside stairs are destroyed. The police and paramedic traffic comes and goes through the outside door. After a while, police officers walk me out, giving me a little assistance. My rib is killing me. Paramedics want to take me to the hospital to check the rib and for observation. I'd rather not.

How the hell am I going to explain this to my dad? This shit makes the bird incident look like a day at the park. Then I make a decision. *Nope. I'm not telling him about this. Even if it makes me Pinocchio for the next several days or for as long as is needed.*

We get to the front of the apartment building. "I want to see Michael,"

I tell the paramedic.

In the hallway, Michael is shaking as he hides behind his mother. She is talking to police.

Several neighbors on the higher floors have come down the stairs—some nosy, some concerned.

I walk over to Michael as he clings to his mother. She looks at me with wariness and shock at my new appearance—the pale skin and darkened eyes. Bending down, I whisper in Michael's ear, "You are going to be okay. That thing is never coming back. You understand me?"

Michael nods. "Besides," I add, "you are like Michael the Archangel. A warrior."

He steps away from his mother and hugs me. It hurts my ribs, but I hug him back, thinking *I need to add Michael and Mrs. Walsh to my Book of Souls.* All the souls that need protection I write in that book. I must come back at some point and check on them, especially because of the other thought on my mind. *You brought this here, Jack—whatever "this" is.*

Detective Gruff and his partner arrive as medical personnel rush Mrs. Walsh into the ambulance. Like everyone else, they are horrified by her condition. Both of them hurry over to me as I continue being examined by the paramedics. They are deeply disturbed by my corpse-like complexion. The Brooklyn police are also circling me.

"Don't let anyone take him anywhere," Detective Gruff barks, leaving me with the more congenial detective.

Immediately, I begin campaigning for them to take me home. "I need to talk to my dad."

The detective walks over to a couple of Brooklyn officers to find out what they know.

Soon, Detective Gruff comes out of the building and walks straight to me. His partner joins us.

"What the hell happened in there? Where was Mrs. Walsh?" he asks, his questions demanding. I close my eyes and begin putting together my own jigsaw puzzle as he follows up with, "Why in God's name did you come to Brooklyn?"

"Alone?" his partner adds.

"Honestly, I can't tell you exactly why I came up here," I reply. "I guess

I just needed to see for myself that Mrs. Walsh wasn't just sitting in her apartment having tea. I needed to know what happened to her."

They wait for more of the story. "She wasn't home," I continue, "and I was about to leave when the little boy across the way, Michael, came out of his apartment and told me she was in the basement."

"Told you?" Detective Gruff asks with a sharp stare. "His mother says he doesn't speak."

"Yes, well, he does a lot of pointing."

I wasn't about to elaborate. Michael may be autistic, but he spoke to me and apparently speaks to Mrs. Walsh. "He, Michael, went into his apartment and came out with a key. I thought it was for the basement, but it was for Mrs. Walsh's apartment. We went in and found a basement key for the outside door," I say.

"The kid told you? Or showed you?" Detective Gruff asks, wanting clarification.

"Yes, in his way. Like I said, he does a lot of pointing."

I cannot be completely honest with them. How can I tell the detectives about my vision regarding Cohen and Philips in the diner without them thinking I was insane? Or that the private detective Peter and I had, Cohen, was selling us out? And what about these intuitive abilities that I have? Not to mention that, yes, the apparently nonverbal kid talked to me.

A Brooklyn detective interrupts us. He looks at Detective Gruff. "You guys are out of your jurisdiction."

"Yes, we know that. We are friends of Jack, here for support," Detective Gruff says. I choose to believe him.

The Brooklyn detective holds two pedestrian drawings. The first is of a Cyclops. "The kid drew this." He shows it to the detectives, then to me. I look at it and then give the detective an expression, like *is there a question attached?*

"How did you get that out of him?" asks Detective Gruff.

"His mother asked him to draw what he saw. He can hear. And see."

They all look at me. "He was big, that's true," I say. "Only I'm pretty sure he had two eyes." That gets a laugh. "Not to be too dramatic, but I was fighting for both of our lives and trying to get the kid out of the basement before he got hurt."

"His mother said he came running into the apartment screaming,"

Detective Gruff says. "She also told us the basement was infested with rats that scared the kid at night."

"If it was a rat that attacked us, Detective, then it was the largest rat I've ever seen. It even walked on two legs," I add, feeling completely in over my head, with no one to turn to for help. Mr. David and the mystics? They crumbled. The nun in the boarding house? *I need her!*

I'm not happy with the fact that I am not supporting Michael's story. I'm making it look like the Cyclops he saw was nothing more than a child's irrational fear. An autistic child at that, whatever comes along with that. Not a proud moment, but who will believe the real story? I convince myself I'm doing it to protect him—and myself.

"How did he escape?" The Brooklyn detective interrupts my internal monologue. "The... whatever it was."

Breathe, Jack, climb that beanstalk, tell your fairytale.

"Not really sure. I'm a little confused because he knocked me around," I say. They are all nodding patiently, but they want an answer. "I think he ran when he heard the sirens."

"Did he run up the stairs?" The Brooklyn detective stares at me. "Into the building?"

"The interior stairs are pretty damaged; could he have made it up those stairs?" counters Detective Gruff.

I think Gruff is throwing me a bone. *Don't lie, Jack, but don't say he crawled into the wall, either.*

"He hit me pretty hard; I was more than a little foggy. But I'm almost positive he did not take the stairs up."

The detective yells to some patrol officers to conduct a full search of the building anyway. He calls over the paramedics and asks if I suffered a concussion in the attack. "Most likely," one of them says.

Great! That's the wave I'm going to ride. Can't remember shit—go with that, Jack.

As I exhale, happy to be off one hook, the Brooklyn detective shows us the second drawing. Although, it is very rough and basic—the scribbles of a young child—it shows clearly enough Mrs. Walsh stuffed in a three-foot jar. It is creepy and accurate.

"What's this?" I ask, the last of my schoolboy innocence on display.

"Thought you could tell us," the Brooklyn detective says.

I stare at Michael's drawing for a long time. His fear is also my fear, a fear we both just lived through and survived—Mrs. Walsh in a pickle jar. The shock is overwhelming.

Might as well tell them the truth. "Yes, the drawing is accurate. Mrs. Walsh was stuffed in a gigantic pickle jar," I say.

All the detectives stare at me, then at the drawing, their faces registering pure disbelief. Chatter ensues, and then the Brooklyn detective turns to me. "How is that possible? And that she's still alive?"

After the paramedic's finish checking me out, they bring me back to the basement. We walk along the outside of the building to the basement stairs. I look for the envelope with the photos of the *Duality* exhibit, hoping it wasn't confiscated by the police. In the midst of the earlier chaos, the Brooklyn detective is realizing they may have trampled on evidence. I walk slowly, looking for a chance to grab the envelope.

They want me to walk them through the attack from the beginning. Where exactly had I found Mrs. Walsh?

"Can I have a moment?" I ask before we walk back into the basement. The detectives move on ahead, giving me a chance to grab the envelope and stick it under my shirt.

When we arrive, we see the forensics team has arrived on-site to dust for fingerprints and take samples.

"Michael came down the stairs," I begin. "We were looking around the basement. I kept telling him she wasn't down here. Michael started to flap his arms, nodding his head and making noises. All of these jars were covered with that canvas. I started poking around, turned some jars around. He started screaming—it was shocking—and I fell back. That's when we were attacked." I am trying with great difficulty not to lie.

"Was he already in the basement or did he come through the outside door?" the detective asks.

"I don't know. I'm not sure. He was just there all of a sudden. It could have happened either way. Michael was insistent and very distracting."

Again, I feel a tinge of guilt. What do you call it when the truth is not enough? I feel like I am throwing Michael under the bus. A kid who is mute, whose life cannot be easy and will never be easy. *What do I do with all of this?*

But I am protecting Michael and myself. We both experienced and witnessed what is rationally not possible, but it is as he has drawn it—a cyclops attacking us and a woman stuffed in a pickle jar. Though, I must tell it in a way they all can believe; I don't make the rules.

The Brooklyn detective wants to know if anybody in the building had a problem with Mrs. Walsh. I know who it is; I know who crawled out of that wall but how do I explain shapeshifting? How do I explain Mr. Philips?

"Can someone get me a fucking aspirin?" I ask while struggling for a way to answer.

The detectives are surprised. By what? That I have a headache? Or that I just said the word 'fuck?' *Give me a break here. First, a mute boy talks to me. Second, I find a woman floating in a large pickle jar. Then, I fight with a Cyclops that is actually… what, a rat? Mr. Philips? Fuck, fuck, fuck!* I start to believe I'm still unconscious from the fall because this is crazier than a make-believe family!

"Can I please have something for my head?" I ask again. "It's about to explode!"

"Let me see if I can get a paramedic."

As the Brooklyn detective leaves, Detective Gruff takes a small bottle of Excedrin from his pocket and hands me two pills. "Go get Jack some water," he says to his partner.

When we are alone, he says, "Look I don't know what the hell happened in here, but you need to be more careful. Stop putting yourself in harm's way."

I nod. "You're right, but on the other hand, we did find Mrs. Walsh."

"Yes… in a jar!" He waits for my reaction. "You saw the shape of that woman. That could have been you. Whoever did that is a psycho and maybe one who plays with the Devil."

Detective Gruff's ability to deliver and understand this bit of information happily surprises me. I think there are people who believe in this—the unseen, the supernatural—and then there are the majority of people who think it's all crazy, imaginary. I would think a detective like Gruff would think people like me are nuts. You know, how everything seems to go back to the insult to my brain. I need someone to believe that we are dealing in the otherworldly. "What happened in there, Jack? Whose story should I believe? Yours? Or the autistic kid's? Because, from the little I've heard about autism, I don't think he knows how to lie."

The detective is correct. It's been a long time since I felt I could tell the truth. I wish it were another way, but it isn't.

"Can you get me home?" I plead, trying to end his inquiry before it gets too far—before I tell him everything. "I'm exhausted, and my father's going to kill me. Maybe it will all come back to me after a good night's sleep."

"Let me see what I can do."

We leave Brooklyn, but I am taken to NYU for observation for a possible concussion as the paramedic suggested. The detectives drive me, which is not protocol, but they come up with a reason that works for Brooklyn PD. Why make this kid's father come out to Brooklyn, especially after he saved a woman's life?

"Not to mention the little kid," Detective Gruff says as he finishes negotiations with Brooklyn PD.

THE HOSPITAL

Dad arrives at the hospital first, followed by Aunt Paula and Uncle Willy, who are both under the influence. They tell me they ran into Brick. Dad is understandably pissed, concerned. He stares at me looking betrayed. "What is it with you, Jack? I don't know what to do with you anymore. It's like you have some kind of death wish." Aunt Paula and Uncle Willy step out of the room.

Detective Gruff becomes my guardian angel. "Mr. Kelly, if I may intrude for just a moment."

Dad spreads his arms and motions with his hands like *please do*. "Sure."

"Don't get me wrong. You have every right to be upset here, but Jack saved a woman's life tonight. And maybe a little boy's as well. If he hadn't gone up there to check on her, she would be dead now. No doubt in my mind. She is in critical condition as we speak. And the..." the detective pauses as if the word he is about to use is not accurate. "...man, who did this to the woman and who attacked the boy—Jack fought him off, for all of their lives."

Dad looks at me with love, but there is also fear in his eyes. A parent may be proud of a child for saving someone, but at the end of the day, they want their own kid home and safely in bed.

"I don't want you to think I'm letting Jack off the hook here. I read him the riot act myself; I told him he should have called me before going to Brooklyn. I told him that there are a lot of bad characters in this world. He didn't run and hide to save himself, and that means something."

"Well, I appreciate that Detective. He… we have had a rough couple of years."

The detective nods his head. "Yes, you have. I know your story." He hands my dad his business card. "Call me if you need anything."

He then turns to me. "Listen to your father; you have a good one."

I could use a joint to calm myself down, but I also know… no more drugs for me. Not even pot. It's been clouding my senses, my abilities. I have to stay alert, ready.

Mr. Philips and I are not finished.

The doctors want to keep me overnight to make sure there is no internal or cranial bleeding. Concern weighs my father down, which makes everything, even the wins, difficult to appreciate.

Finally, Dad and I are alone. "Dad, I'm fine. I feel great. This is just bullshit," I say.

"Well, I'm going to stay."

"No. You're not staying. This is not like the last time. I'm okay; you taught me how to take care of myself. You know all that exercise you made me do after the fall and the rope down the middle of the apartment? It paid off tonight."

He fusses but leaves reluctantly.

Falling asleep is easy but staying asleep is hard. I hear the sound of someone walking slowly down the hall, a telephone ringing, a voice in prayer, a chorus of chants. There is a lot going on, and it's not just in my head. I wake up. The phone must be Dad saying goodnight. I don't pick it up. *Who is praying? Chanting?*

The sound of the footsteps grows louder and louder. There are no lights on in the room or hall. I lay in total darkness.

The noise keeps getting louder. *Damn! The phone won't stop ringing.*

Suddenly, everything goes silent, except the telephone. The footsteps stop. Someone stands outside my room.

The door slowly opens. Pulling myself up, I realize someone is also sitting in the chair next to my bed. The telephone continues to ring.

"Don't let him in, Jack."

I look slowly to my left. The nun from the boarding house sits in the chair next to my bed. My mouth flies open, full of shock. This is the first time she has come to me.

I return my attention to the doorway. A small ray of moonlight reveals Mr. Philips standing there with a deep, nasty cut that oozes in the center of his forehead. The location of the mystical Third Eye... or, for a Cyclops, the only eye.

The phone continues to ring. "Answer it," the nun whispers.

I must still be dreaming, but I do as I'm told. "Hello?"

"Jack? You haven't left yet?"

"Um, no." I'm completely confused, but something in the dream is familiar.

"You had a migraine, right?"

"Katherine?" *Katherine? How is this happening? All the doctors told me it was the brain injury... that I imagined her—my wife—and my kids; the fall created all that. How can she be calling me here in the hospital while I'm still a fifteen-year-old boy?*

"Come home, Jack. I have your dinner in the oven. The kids are waiting for you."

I don't know whether to smile, laugh, or cry. "Oh, Katherine, it's so good to hear your voice."

"Jack, did you have a couple of drinks?" Moment of panic. I remember this. She called me. Stevie is sick.

"No. Just a migraine. Is everyone... is everything okay?" I ask, hesitating on almost every word. *Am I talking to a ghost?*

"Everyone, everything is fine."

I look around the room. No longer am I lying in a hospital bed. Instead, I'm sitting in my office in Los Angeles. It is all coming back to me.

"How's Stevie?"

"Sitting here doing his homework. Want to say hello?"

"Yes!"

Stevie gets on the phone. "Hey, Dad, I'm working on this cross pass in soccer; I want you to help me this weekend."

"You got it. Stevie, how you feeling?"

"I'm great, Dad!"

"How are Lily and Mikey?"

"Everyone is fine, Dad. We are all just sitting here doing homework, waiting for you."

"Great, I'm on my way." I hang up the telephone and head out of the office.

When I walk into my house, everything is just as I left it. The kids are all healthy, and Katherine is moving about happily, as if nothing ever happened. She puts a plate on the table. It's one of my favorites—Chicken Cordon Bleu.

"Did you get the Midrin?" she asks.

"Yes," I lie.

"They delivered the safe. It's in the garage."

I'm trying hard to catch up. It's quite a gap between a fifteen-year-old boy in the hospital and a forty-seven-year old husband and father of three. *Why do I want a safe?*

"Oh. Okay."

"Jack, some guy called today asking about a painting."

"What?" My entire body shakes. I feel like I'm coming out of my skin. *How can I protect my family? This is never ending…*

"He said he was a curator at a small museum downtown that is doing a retrospective on a Kasper Greenstreet. He wanted to see if you might be interested in selling a painting of his that you own?"

I try to answer her but cannot. I feel myself caught in the in-between.

"I must say I laughed," she continues. "Can you imagine us owning a Kasper Greenstreet original? All three of our kids' college educations would be paid for."

It feels like a train is running through the middle of my chest. I struggle to blurt it out. "Did he give you his name?"

"Yes. Wait a minute, let me get it…"

My heart is racing. I am no longer there, apparently—or maybe I am, or both, the in-between—

but I can sense Mr. Philips continues moving into my hospital room.

"Seymore Hunter," she says, her voice fading…

I glance away from Katherine and am back to the hospital; I look away from the phone to see the nun firmly blocking the door. She is facing him.

Her back is to me, blocking my ability to see Mr. Philips. She is praying with great force in Latin. "Put on the full armor of God so that you can take your stand against the Devil's schemes. For our struggle is not flesh and blood but against the rulers, against the authorities, against the powers of the dark world, and against the spiritual forces of evil in the heavenly realms. Therefore, put on the full armor of God so that when the day of evil comes you may be able to stand your ground..."

I look at my hand, hoping that I'm still holding my fork at the dinner table with Katherine and my kids. Instead, it is holding the telephone receiver, and I am sitting in my hospital bed.

"Seymore Hunter?" I repeat.

Suddenly, the nun is blown back into the chair with incredible power and force. "Don't let him in, Jack!" she yells.

If she can't stop him, how can I?

I get out of bed and walk slowly to the door. Mr. Philips' face is not the same. The hole in the middle of his forehead is now an open, expanding wound, oozing all kinds of secretion. His eyes, however, maintain that icy blue color.

"Seymore Hunter, the painting is not for sale," I say, now realizing that he and Philips are one and the same.

For some reason, reciting that name I'd never heard before prevents him from entering my room, but I know it is a momentary sedative. I close the door in his face.

I turn to the nun. Her voice is urgent, reminding me of our first meeting when I fell through the floor in the boarding house. "Go back to your body. Don't let them attach to you. You must be very careful, Jack. That is pure evil!" Our connection is heart to heart, telepathic. There are no words said aloud.

"Can he hear us?"

"No."

"What can I do?"

"You must find out what he needs in the painting and use it against him," she says. "It's not enough to hide it. He will never stop looking for it until he gets it!"

THE PAINTING

The warehouse is quiet when I arrive. I feel alone and paranoid as I unlock the door to our storage container. While unwrapping the painting, I stare at Kasper Greenstreet's actual child subject. It is clearly me. I see it in an obvious way I never saw the first few times that I viewed the painting. Nothing has moved; the painting has sat in its wrapper just as I left it. I begin to touch the very expensive painting, hoping to understand and even control its mystical elements. I outline the shadows with my fingers, certain these are the things Mr. Philips—Seymore Hunter or whatever his name is—wants. I'm a witness to their power.

I decide to try and command them to move, to step out of the painting. I want to see them in action. The way they were in Kasper's apartment.

"Slide out!"

I step back, waiting for the show to begin. Nothing. "Show yourself. Come dance on the wall."

The sound of an elevator in the distance makes me pause, makes me edgy. I sit in the small storage space, studying the painting, remaining quiet. Again, I trace the shadows and study the painting. I know its magic, its source of power. The silence is deafening. I wait for some kind of explosion.

Nothing. I sit and then meditate. The words of the nun echo in my head: "You must find out what he needs in the painting."

One more time, I ask the shadows to oblige me. "I've seen you in the hospital room, in the subway. I've watched you move, slither from the painting, slide up the walls in Kasper's apartment. Reveal yourself to me."

Again, nothing happens. Surely, they are remaining still because I do not possess the power to make them move. Now I feel ridiculous. I decide to rewrap the painting, but before doing so, I trace the child with my fingers, watching the shadows for any hint of movement.

They are still.

A moment later, though, I feel a sudden current, a movement of energy in my hands. As I step back to view the full painting, I realize the image of the child has moved. He is no longer looking down at the marbles but facing me.

It scares the shit out of me. With it, I can now feel and hear my blood moving through my body. By looking at myself as a child staring back at me, it changes the entire landscape of the image and the painting. It no longer feels like an object of art. It becomes a living, breathing, moving thing. The day at Madison Square Park comes back to me. I remember the marbles, the feeling of being watched. Apparently by Kasper Greenstreet, as the painting shows, but also by something else, other beings or forces. God, for sure. But something else…

"Jack?" I whisper. Who am I whispering to? The image in a painting?

He has some damage. An insult to the brain.

But not on that day. That was long before my fall, my injury. Yet, I still felt something otherworldly.

I place both my hands on the painted image of me, feeling crazy. "I know you moved. Can you help me?" I humbly ask.

"How?" the response comes in the voice of a child.

My heart threatens to jump out of my chest. I look around the room to make sure I am alone. "What are you?" I ask.

"A boy."

"No. You are a boy in a painting," I say.

"Yes, but still a boy," he replies.

"But who—or what—are you?"

"You," he says.

I step back from the painting as far as I can in the small storage space. He now stands tall on the canvas, the marbles at his feet.

This is all demonic to be sure. Everything is making me leery. I gather enough courage to ask, "What should I call you?"

"Jack."

"But who are you? What are you?"

"Yourself." I think I know what he means, but I must be sure.

"You mean… you are me?"

He bends down and picks up a marble, stands tall again, and offers it to me. My brain and body scream to be cautious. The blood in my veins moves like a wild river. It lights me up with a feeling, a sensation, an emotion that I have never felt before. It is as if worlds collide. The living and the dead. The past and the future. For a fleeting moment, I question myself. *Did I bring something evil back with me after the fall when I returned to my body? Did something attach to me?* He stands in place, holding his marble.

"You know, I had—we—had an accident." He looks at me in a peculiar way. "It was after this painting of you—of me."

He again offers the marble to me.

Before I take the marble, I must be sure. "What do you know about these shadows? The shadows in this painting?"

"They've done some bad things."

"Yes, that I know," I say.

"They're not mine," he quickly adds.

"No, I didn't think so; they're not ours," I reach out slowly towards him and pull the marble out of his hand and out of the painting. The feel and the look of the marble in my hand causes me to remember being a boy. I caress its smooth body in my hand while a tear runs down my face.

"Are you stuck in there?" I ask, trying to fight back the tears.

"No."

"Can they hurt you?" The tears keep coming, but I don't know why.

"I told you, the shadows are not mine. They won't be hurting anyone anymore."

I start to wipe away my tears. "How do you know?"

"Because the man who the shadows belonged to is gone," he says.

"Kasper?"

"I'm not sure of his name, but I knew him, and he is gone."

"How can you be sure they won't do bad things again?"

"Because they were lonely and afraid. They were shadow-less, in a sense."

"Are you sure?" I ask.

"How can you be a shadow if the person whose shadow you belong to is gone?"

The boy—the painted boy version of me—makes a good point. "And now, what are they?"

"Now they belong to me!" he says, as though they are innocent little puppies.

He tosses another marble out of the painting. One of the shadows slithers out behind it, picks up the marble, and jumps back into the canvas with the happiness of a dog fetching a bone.

I'm blown away.

After a moment, I sit cross-legged, Sukhasana style. He does the same. We talk about everything that he remembers. The Jack in the painting—Yourself, as he's asked me to call him— reminds me that he—we—heard voices and picked up on different energies long before my fall. He also reminds me that he is not stuck in the painting. He compares it to being in the hand of God, with no fear, pain, or sorrow. However, he is completely aware of all the chaos and sadness that the painting and shadows helped to create. Now, though, he is in complete control of the shadows, which he proves in various ways. He has the shadows move away from him in the painting, giving him space.

The Jack in the painting—Yourself—plays the game "Simon Says." All three shadows follow his instructions. One shadow picks up three marbles and juggles them. Another shadow does a handstand. They are not menacing at all, which is mystifying, because I know what they have done and what they are capable of doing. The shadows are completely at his command. It is a circus but a child's circus. And he shows his control in loving, respectful ways. It is soothing because I know Yourself is all about love, and he is using this love to teach the shadows that the hauntings will not continue.

I stay with the Jack in the painting well into the night. He reminds me of the many things I have forgotten, along with something that is very urgent and important: the injury to my brain did not bring the supernatural world to me, like I've thought all along. Instead, he says, it was always there for us.

We talk about Kasper Greenstreet, the man who created the painting, and the shadows. He tells me how the shadows were able to leave the storage area in the Gramercy Terrace apartment building when Kasper called on them.

Before I leave, I tell him about Mr. Philips/Seymore Hunter, his eagerness to possess the painting, and his wickedness.

"When doing research on Kasper, it was said that he used blood in his paintings," I say. "That it gave him some kind of artistic power, the ability to make magic."

Yourself is aware of Mr. Philips. "There is blood in the painting," he says. "I've seen him smell it, look for it."

"Do you know what in the painting has the blood mixed with it?"

"Yes. Everything." Long pause. "Except for me. The man thinks that's what controls the shadows. The blood," Yourself says.

"And it doesn't?"

"Not anymore. I told you, they belong to me now."

I quickly make a habit of going to the storage unit every day to visit Yourself. On my third visit, we talk again about Mr. Philips/Seymore Hunter and what to do about him. A little later, Yourself tells me not to come back so often, which surprises me and leaves me more than a little sad. Another loss.

"It's not that I don't like seeing you," he says. "It's just the way it should be."

Before I leave, he gets back into his original position—kneeling on one knee, playing with his marbles.

Walking home, I feel a sense of joy and a sense of loss. He asked me not to come back so often which is obviously a loss, but I feel as if I have found myself—my earlier self. My true self. Yourself told me it wasn't the fall that created these so-called abilities that I have; they were there from the beginning. I—we—had these supernatural gifts as a child.

If the fall didn't create my supernatural abilities, it couldn't have created Katherine and the kids…

My happiness disappears when I think of Philips. He is the one who has the Polaroid pictures; he is the one with the list of people that own the other Kasper Greenstreet paintings. I sense—know—that he wants to find out if the other paintings have any power he can use or if they are just art hanging on collectors' walls.

Mr. Philips has a way of getting into places. And there is nothing in any of the paintings that has power of its own. There is the blood, of course, but blood must be mixed with something evil or mystical, and there is only one painting with that. The self-portrait of Kasper Greenstreet as a child, the one with the shadows. And I am in possession of that painting.

I dread that everything hangs in the balance. Katherine. My kids. The life I know and will know. Philips knows it is I that is keeping the painting from him. Killing me I fear will be his pleasure.

Brick and I walk down 23rd Street, looking for an underground alley to smoke a joint in. The underground alleys are an amazing way to travel without being seen, and we are definitely not looking for attention. We can walk all the way up to 29th Street without coming above ground. Brick lights a joint as soon as we descend the stairs and takes a long hit.

"Do you believe in the supernatural?" I ask.

"You mean like ghosts and shit?" A puzzled look crosses his face.

"Yeah, like ghosts, voodoo, witches."

Brick nods. "You know Miguel's mother practices Santeria? He says she can put spells on people."

He hands me the joint, but I hand it back without taking a hit. "Why, Jack? You seeing ghosts?" he asks.

Philips has me in his sights before I have a chance to pick up on his energy. My loud pulsating energy is easy to find, and Philips follows Brick and I into the underbelly of the tenement buildings.

Everything is moving inside me. My blood races through my veins; it's my warning shot, my alarm, and it tells me all I need to know. We are not alone.

Brick stops in mid-toke. "What is it?"

A cat trails us. I immediately know what that means. I turn around and begin to chase it, but it turns and hisses at me. Two more cats appear.

I'm nervous. "Let's put the joint out and go up to the street." I don't want Brick to get caught in the middle, especially down here.

"You're just paranoid," Brick says. "The pot will relax you; it always does."

"No. I need my wits about me."

At the end of the alley, I see the outline of a large man. My mind races to the thought of Philips turning into a Cyclops, but now we're in an alley, not a basement.

Brick and I start to run. A screeching sea of feral cats greets us. I run right through them as they try to attack my legs. Brick stops, puzzled, before he quickly follows.

Back on 23rd Street, I now see Philips waiting for me. The only pleasure I get in seeing him is the oozing indentation in his Third Eye, which came from me.

"Jack. What's the matter?" Brick yells. "Is this guy bothering you?!" His tone is of a loud, aggressive, threatening teenager.

Mr. Philips does not fear teenage kids, with or without powers. He is a hunter through and through. He lets out a roar and growls at Brick in a chilling, wolf-like manner.

We take off running. He follows us in the many forms he can take on—first, a large rat that appears to have wings growing from its back. It runs along the sidewalk, before it transforms into a raven flying just above us like enemy aircraft. Brick runs down the stairs into the subway. I follow, worried about bringing him into this mess. Brick runs along the platform and jumps on a train that's ready to leave the station. I jump on right behind him.

"What the fuck was that?" Brick screams. His voice is high pitched, hardly recognizable. He is visibly shaken.

Before I have a chance to answer, Philips walks through the subway car, directly at us. His face changes to half-wolf, half-human. A werewolf. He bares his teeth and begins growling in a deep, guttural manner, which scares the shit out of everyone in the car. People fold over themselves and climb on to the seats. Brick and I run. We head through the gangway to the corridor—the area between cars. Philips changes form constantly and uses deep claws to leave scratch marks in his wake, while howling and making other ear-piercing animal sounds.

The lights in the train go off and on.

Brick and I stay ahead of him until we reach the last car. We have nowhere left to go. Brick fights with the rear door, trying like hell to get it open. Philips steps into the car just as Brick breaks the door with the fire extinguisher. We are at the end of the train, which is slowing down as it begins pulling into the station.

"We need to jump!" I yell. "We need to jump!"

We jump onto the tracks. Philips stands at the rear door, letting out a roar that vibrates through the tunnel. His roar brings out the skeletal horse-head creatures, which begin their own guttural howling.

"What the fuck! What the fuck's happening?!" Brick screams, on the verge of a full meltdown.

Philips leaps into the air, changing into what appears to be an albino bat. He then metamorphoses into several different creatures before landing on the tracks as an oversized rat.

I grab Brick's hand. We run along the tracks as a train approaches from the opposite direction. "Brick, stay close to me!" The train horn blasts as we cling to the wall. We vibrate from both the sound and movement of the oncoming train. Brick pisses himself.

After the train passes, one of the skeletal creatures faces us. "You don't know if you are a man or horse, so I'll treat you like a dog!" I yell.

It stops. I grab its tail and swing it with all my might toward the rat. It's not as easy as the nun made it look.

Brick runs down the tracks to the end of a platform and climbs up. He starts to run but turns back to help me up. As I get to my feet, Philips changes from the oversized rat to his own human form except for Medusa-like snakes slithering from his arms. He grabs hold of Brick, stunning him, then wraps himself around Brick's neck, chest, and legs like a serpent. The roaring of another approaching train drowns out Brick's screams for help.

"Please! Please let him go!" I yell. "I have what you want!"

Philips smiles at my weakness as I take out the key to the storage. Not the least bit worried about whatever abilities I may have.

"I'll give you the painting! I know it's the blood and the shadows you want!"

Brick is confused and horrified. Philips dangles him off the platform as the train gets closer and closer. I hold the key up over my head. "Seymore Hunter! I'll take you there!"

A transit cop has quietly slid along the wall to help us. Philips already is aware of this, and I become aware by watching his reaction. "What the fuck!?" the transit cop yells as he sees all the snakes coming out of Philips' body.

When the train arrives, Philips tosses Brick into a pillar knocking him out. He then grabs hold of the transit officer, tossing him into the oncoming train and to his death.

Before I can react, Philips wraps his serpent arms around my leg, neck, and arm, immobilizing me. There is no escape.

He firmly leads me up the stairs and out of the subway. The snakes tighten their grip as we begin to walk slowly to the storage unit and the painting. While walking down 23rd Street, it feels like we are alone, not surrounded by the mass of people like on any day in Manhattan. They are all around us, yet do not see us.

We arrive at the storage unit. Once inside, he takes the key from my hand and very slowly opens the storage door. *I have failed; all is lost.* I know I will never make it out of the storage unit alive.

Philips shoves me inside and follows me into the cramped area. The painting leans against the wall, just as I left it. Philips' body has returned to its natural state; the Medusa-like serpent arms are now gone, but he is still intimidating.

He gives me an eerie smile. "Unwrap it," he orders.

I do as I am told. His body begins to shine; it is a yellow eerie light. Philips pushes me out of the way and kneels before the painting, then leans in to smell it. Right away, he senses the blood. His licks the painting with his tongue, which is not a normal human tongue.

Smiling, he touches the shadows. "Dance for me," he commands.

They don't move. He smells them again. "You know who I am." He utters it as a statement, not a question. "Come and show me what you can do."

Nothing. He turns to me, his blue eyes piercing and frightening, vengeance on his mind. "What did you do to them that has made them so docile?"

"I didn't do anything."

Philips smacks me into the wall and bares his teeth. *What is with this guy?* Then he turns back to the painting. His face changes colors and shapes. Demonic, for sure.

"I will kill you here. I will sacrifice you to the power of this painting!" he barks in a multitude of distorted voices, which scares the hell out of me. He turns to face me. "This is where you die, Jack Kelly."

"Mister..." Yourself says from the painting.

Philips turns back to the source of the voice, the painting. Yourself is facing him, which surprises Philips. I can't tell if it is a happy surprise or if he has been caught completely off guard. I know he is here for the shadows and the blood, not this sideshow.

"Want to play marbles?"

While Philips puzzles over the question, Yourself fires a marble at the center of Philips' forehead, where it sticks into the open wound. Philips' natural eyes pop out as he begins to alter his body. Before he gets very far, three shadows grab hold of him and begin to pull him into the painting—the last thing he expected or prepared for. They suck the top half of his body into the painting with a giant gulping sound. In equally spectacular fashion, his legs begin to change into many forms, some that I cannot identify.

Moments later, a vortex seems to open in the painting. With a vile screeching sound, Philips is gone, inhaled by the painting. Smothered between the three shadows.

I sit in place, stunned and in shock. After a bit, I crawl over to the painting. There is a tiny spot of silver hair between the shadows—the last remnant of Philips. The painting returns to the way it was, with Yourself and the marbles in front of him. The shadows stand above, no longer menacing. It becomes clear to me the shadows do belong to the boy in the painting now.

Still, I need to clear something up with Yourself. "You told me you would not let the shadows move when Philips came. You said you wanted him to see they weren't useful." He doesn't answer. "Jack? Yourself?"

I begin to rewrap the painting. Yourself smiles and turns his head ever so slightly. "Don't worry. The man had evil intentions. He was going to hurt you. I couldn't let him do that. Now he can't hurt anyone."

"What about you? Are you stuck with him, with them now?" I ask.

"No. As I said, I'm very happy here. This is my painting, and they belong to me."

I touch his image very gently, and he goes back to his pose. I think of something I heard once but can't remember from where or who exactly—school maybe; Mr. David; or Hermes, the herald of the Grecian gods. "As above so below, as within, so without, as the Universe, so the soul."

HOME

I touch the boy in the portrait, as I always do on the rare occasions I visit with the painting. I hope that he will move, acknowledge my presence. But he doesn't. Nothing has changed in the painting since that day in New York when Yourself outfoxed Mr. Philips/Seymore Hunter and lured him into the canvas.

Katherine and I place the painting into the new safe that has just been delivered, lock it, and get back to our lives.

It is a typical day in the Kelly house, normal as any other any day. Katherine and I have explained to our kids that they must never display or sell the painting. I have not told them everything, but I have told them enough. They understand that not all things are good.

We go about our daily lives like ordinary people. The gifts or abilities that I possessed and used as a child followed me into adulthood, and I can see them developing in my kids. Every once in a while, though, something commands our attention, something that could be considered otherworldly… if you believe in that sort of thing.

ABOUT THE AUTHOR

Kevin Moore is the author of *The Book of Souls*, a mystical ghost story, it is his first novel and the first book in the series featuring Jack Kelly and his paranormal abilities. *The Book of Demons* (think Harry Potter meets the Exorcist) is the sequel to *The Book of Souls*. Moore also wrote *Christmas Stories 7 Original Short Stories* which is available everywhere. His play *Conversations From The Sports Arena* was performed at the HBO Theater in Hollywood. He also had his first children's picture book *Me and My Shadow* released in 2021. Moore hopes to continue the Jack Kelly paranormal saga in a third book which he is currently working on. Moore practices Lucid Dreaming which has helped him with his writing. He is a Yogi and an Advanced Reiki Practitioner—most importantly he is Matthew and Madison's father.

THE
END

Made in United States
North Haven, CT
05 November 2022

26328025R00088